THE MAN
WHO WROTE
DIRTY BOOKS

THE MAN
WHO WROTE
DIRTY BOOKS

HAL DRESNER

OPEN ROAD

INTEGRATED MEDIA

NEW YORK

Copyright © 1964 by Hal Dresner

ISBN 978-1-4976-4493-9

This edition published in 2014 by Open Road Integrated Media, Inc.
345 Hudson Street
New York, NY 10014
www.openroadmedia.com

TO MY SISTER REA
WITH LOVE AND PRIDE
AND EVERYTHING ELSE

NOVEMBER 2

FROM BENJAMIN WINK, SCEPTER BOOKS,
NEW YORK CITY

October 31

Dear Mase—Just a note to forward the enclosed letter. They can say what they like about Scepter but they can't say we open mail to our writers. Hope it's good news, boy. I sit here at my desk and the pages of my calendar blow off like in the movies. Today is October, tomorrow is November, then it's December and time to set up your new book. When can we expect it? *This Flogged Flesh* is moving fine although it's too early to tell. But I know it will do as well as *Damned by Desire* or *Bare with Me.* You've got something that makes the others look like the hacks they are and your readers know it. I was talking to someone from K & G and he said, "Guy LaDouche, Guy LaDouche, Guy LaDouche." He can't keep you in stock fast enough. And don't think it's just the covers we give you either, because that airbrush job Art did on *Damned* was the worst possible. As you rightly said, it looked like the girl had 2% breasts. But the book still sold better than any other. I only wish our mystery line was doing half as well. We got better than 30% returns on *Death in Pink Panties* and *A Bra Full of Bullets,* not to mention what happened with that science-fiction thing, *The Green Lovers.* Did you get the copies of *Flogged* I sent last week? I spent a week in Vermont once and none of my mail reached me. Let me know if you didn't get them and well put a tracer on it. Frankly, I don't know why you want to stay up there in the boondocks now that summer is over in the first place. You could write just as well from an apartment here and have the whole city to get ideas from. But I've been in this business one way or another long enough to know you can't argue with artists, so have it your own way. Just wanted you to know you're welcome. Did you finish your Serious Book yet? What's it all about? If it's not done, don't get discouraged, because those things take time. I can't wait to read your latest for us. Hit them where they live, fella!

Ben

ENCLOSURE FROM BENJAMIN WINK

66 Lemming Lane
Sacasas 4, Ill.
29 October

Mr. "Guy LaDouche"
c/o Scepter Books
P.O. Box 85388
New York City, N.Y.

Sir:

I trust it will come as no surprise to learn that my daughter, Barbara Victoria, is suing you in the amount of $100,000 for the crime of libel. My attorneys will be in contact with you to present the particulars, but I wish to take this opportunity to express my personal contempt and loathing.

Should you be as failing in memory as you are in all the other qualities which distinguish man from the lower animals, I am referring to the vile passages on pages 104–138 of your book, *This Flogged Flesh,* wherein you relate an alleged liaison between one Hartley Young and a lady whom you have the audacity to identify as Bibbsy Dibbs. Were you only guilty of mentioning my daughter's name in such context, I might be persuaded to dismiss the incident as coincidence. But your repeatedly exact and tasteless descriptions of her—including a base allusion to a mark on a portion of her anatomy which my dignity as a father forbids me to mention—display such an indisputable intent to malign as cannot go unpunished.

My attorneys inform me that if I so desire I may also take action for defamation against you on behalf of my late wife and myself for references to us (page 126) as "a dipsomaniac ex-manicurist" and "a deranged Naval officer." At this time, however, despite the fact that your biography indicates you are forty years my junior and I am partially incapacitated, I would prefer to take my satisfaction by horsewhipping you to your knees at the first opportunity.

The method by which you obtained private knowledge of my family is presently unknown to me. My daughter does not recall having encountered you under your present nom de plume. However, the events you evoke remind her of Jim or Jack Ferguson, whom she met at Cape Cod two summers ago, and/or Vince Delatorre, whose acquaintance she made in New Orleans in 1958. Whichever of these is your real name, or the name under which you were masquerading at the time, be assured that I shall find you out.

During my thirty-two years of military service I had many "literary persons" under my command. To a man I found them to be spineless, lazy, uncooperative drunkards with a marked disdain for anyone otherwise employed. Nevertheless, they did serve their country whereas I notice no mention of military service in your biography.

I sincerely hope that the others who have suffered from your black pen will instigate legal and personal steps such as those which I anticipate with great relish. I wish them the greatest success.

Yours truly,
Lt. Commander E. B. Dibbs, USN
(Ret.)

NOVEMBER 3

TO LT. COMMANDER E. B. DIBBS, SACASAS, ILL.

P.O. Box 15
Camphor, Vermont
Nov 3

Dear Sir:

Your letter of Oct 29 has just been forwarded to me by my publisher. It has led me to believe you are an imaginary personality created by Dave Noodleman and/or Monty Shregossin.

As one hack to another, boys, you blew it by having Dibbs refer to the birthmark on Bibbsy's butt. In keeping with the old bastard's dignified front, I doubt if he'd mention such an intimate characteristic, especially in a letter to a man he was planning to horsewhip. But the horsewhipping idea was nice, probably just what the anachronistic old seahorse would think of. And the Jim or Jack Ferguson and Vince Delatorre were inspired names. They summon up visions of a clubby Back Bay dilettante and a stud dockworker which in turn provide some sweet insights into Barbara Victoria. I'd guess that Monty, as an experienced wastrel, came up with Ferguson while Dave, if only to substantiate his wild boasts, is responsible for the stud. Both of you could probably make a good buck writing nasty books and if you re interested, there's an empty cabin right down the mountain. The trees are so intimidating that you'll never miss the cities; the air is so pure that on a windy day you can smell Hartford and liquor is fair-traded. (Although, so help me, I haven't had a gargle in months.) I picked this place with a map, a dart and a blindfold, feeling that if chopping wood and burning garbage made men out of Buddha, Christ and Thoreau, it was just the ticket for me. But so far the only garbage I've burned has been 120 pages of a book that was destined to make my name in American letters. Among the garbage I have not burned has been *In Naked Tempest, Cash in Passion, Summer Sinners* (some are not) and *Vices of the Vikings,* an historical.

For all of that, my sole roommate was a schoolteacher from Amy Jo Spod Elementary, North Highland, N.J., who rented a nearby cottage by mail under the impression she could hear the Tanglewood Festival from her porch. She was not a geography teacher. When she arrived and discovered her error, her landlord refused to refund her deposit and she was forced by finances to remain. I accosted her in the post office. (I have never been much for cunning ways to meet people.) She was a frailish thing, though not so easily blown about as it might seem. After her first month was up, she moved in with me. Again it was a matter of money. We had no sex together. She preferred it thus unless I felt I loved her "at least a little." That, I believe, was a line she read somewhere and immediately adopted as a makeshift chastity belt. If I admitted to loving her a trifle, I think she would have used that to keep me in hand. She seemed delighted to wear her scarlet letter in the village while remaining Miss Dove with me. I was discontent with continence but the bargain seemed not bad enough to break. (In my youth, Father William, I often believed/ That platonic affairs were the best,/ But now as I age, I grow rather sage/ And see them as inactive incest.) A week before she left we became genuinely fond of each other. But then, of course, it was too late to bring personalities into it. We promised not to write and I've kept my word. I hope I never see her again.

On the subject, this is my eighth month of celibacy. A record for the club, I believe. There was a brief affair in N.Y. with a girl who worked for a trampoline manufacturer, but naturally she was much in demand. Before that, a hiatus of almost four months. I believe that writing pornography vicariously dulls one's sex life. I keep expecting my partners to have flanks like golden ramparts and breasts like cannon shells. Everyone seems flabby nowadays.

So, if you are coming up, better empty your cups before you arrive because once the snow starts there's not even a Kodiak around. Bastard, my weimaraner, is beginning to complain of the inactivity already and we're not due to get the season's first flurry for another month —according to the Camphor climatologist, who is also the postmaster and package store owner, and who has called every snowfall, presidential election and Miss Rheingold winner in the past fifty years. He's also my landlord and has warned me of the danger of getting snowbound or going nuts. Nobody has ever passed a winter in this cabin before. When I heard that, of course I had to stay. Who was it, after all, that conquered the challenge of Blenda Koblensky? (Does that name set me hopping with passion! If only they didn't grow up.)

Anyway, it was good to hear from you and to know that you picked up one of my trashics and found someone to read it to you. Don't wait for the next one before you write again. My best to Cora, Bonnie and your thousand children.

Mase

P.S. Who the hell do you know in Sacasas, Ill. to act as a middleman?

NOVEMBER 5

FROM BENJAMIN WINK

November 3

Dear Mase—Just a note to forward the enclosed letter which came today. Looks official. Did you get my note with an enclosed letter I sent a few days ago? How's the new book coming? Any title yet? We're starting a new Americana series. Bill has already finished *Manhattan Madam* and Larry signed up for *Bible Belt Bawd.* Comster is running it and I don't know what he's paying but when it comes to pirating writers from the same house, I didn't think they could pay a real writer enough. We've started to get some returns of Kenny's book, *Of Beastly Lust.* Only about 1100 so far, but I have the feeling it's just the start. I told him that barnyard stuff wouldn't go but he had to have it his way. Now he says it's the cover that killed it. As if he didn't know as well as I that Art slaved his heart out over that cover. How many ways can you draw a sheep? On top of that, I think they may ban it in South Dakota. Well, better they get us on a poor book than one of yours, I say. Keep punching, boy!

Ben

ENCLOSURE FROM BENJAMIN WINK

Berry, Lock & Gru
Attorneys at Law
1136 Michigan Avenue
Chicago, Illinois

Mr. Guy LaDouche
c/o Scepter Books
P.O. Box 85388
Grand Central Station
New York City, N.Y.

November 1

Re: Dibbs vs. LaDouche a/k/a Ferguson
a/k/a Delatorre

Dear Mr. LaDouche:
I trust by this time you have received a letter from our client, Lt. Commander E. B. Dibbs, USN (Ret), informing you of his daughters intent to instigate a defamation action against you. In the event you have not yet received that letter, the enclosed complaint will acquaint you with the particulars of the suit.

In the hope of avoiding the embarrassment to all parties which a court hearing would entail, I would suggest you have your attorney contact me at the first opportunity to negotiate a satisfactory private settlement.

Yours truly,

mnbv Quentin L. Gru

QLG:cj
Enc.
cc: Lt. Commander E. B. Dibbs

NOVEMBER 6

TO BENJAMIN WINK

Nov 6

Dear Ben:
Thanks for the notes of Oct 31 and Nov 3 and the enclosed letters which were just an elaborate joke by some friends. Thanks also for the copies of *Flogged* which I did receive. Art outdid himself on the cover, except that the man appears to be shooting the girl with a whip.

My Serious Book has run into difficulties. I burned it last week. It was to be a novelistic treatment of the case proving that Shakespeare and Dickens were one and the same. (Next time you read *Dombey and Son,* see if the old man doesn't remind you of Guildenstern.) I'm getting down to my proper calling today and should have the new one to you by Dec 10 at the latest. No title as yet.

I agree with you completely about the new Americana series. If a writer can't preserve his loyalty in this business, then what can he keep?

Bad luck on *Of Beastly Lust.* Maybe Kenny should do another book on fetishism. I thought *Passions Fashions* was one of his finest.

All best.

Mase

NOVEMBER 7

FROM LT. COMMANDER E. B. DIBBS

5 November

Sir:

I am in receipt of your letter of 3 November which I have turned over to my attorneys. They are of the opinion that it constitutes new defamation of me. For this reason I have instructed them to accept no settlement less than $250,000.

Your letter describes you as an even more opprobrious person than I thought possible. It will be only by a great effort of will that I shall halt at horsewhipping when first we meet. A more fitting reward for your calumny would be to throw you to the sharks with whose barbarous nature you have displayed such a kinship. I am considering contacting the principal of Amy Jo Spod Elementary School in order to inform your former paramour of your braggadocio and suggest this revenge to her.

Your new pseudonym has failed to confuse my daughter. She believes she had the misfortune to encounter you in January, 1960, at the Maharajah Hotel in Miami Beach, Florida, where you were allegedly employed as a beach boy under the name of Bart Chernow.

> Yours truly,
> *Lt. Commander E. B. Dibbs, USN*
> *(Ret.)*

NOVEMBER 8

TO LT. COMMANDER E. B. DIBBS

Nov 8

Dear Sir:

I am in receipt of your letter of Nov 5 as well as the letter and enclosed complaint from your attorneys dated Nov 1.

First, let me repeat that I am still of the opinion that this entire affair is a joke being sponsored by my friends. Or those who imagine themselves friends of mine. If this is not the case, however, and I am corresponding with a real person named Lt. Commander E. B. Dibbs, who has the actual grievances detailed, let me offer my sincere apologies for any confusion my previous reply may have caused you. If you will put yourself in my situation, sir—the situation of a reclusive writer with an assortment of inveterate pranksters for friends—you may find my responses understandable and excusable.

Furthermore, if I am addressing a real Lt. Commander Dibbs, I wish to state emphatically that to the best of my knowledge, prior to receiving your letter of Oct 29, I have never known of the existence of a Barbara or Bibbsy Dibbs, an E. B. Dibbs, or any of their relatives either living or dead. The Dibbses mentioned in my book were completely manufactured by my imagination and their resemblance to any real persons either living or dead is purely coincidental.

I believe if you will look at the front of my book, you will find a printed statement which makes substantially this same claim.

Furthermore, my real name is Mason Clark Greer and the only nom de plume I have ever employed is Guy LaDouche. I have never been to Cape Cod or New Orleans and can, if necessary, produce evidence of my whereabouts elsewhere during the periods of my alleged presence in those areas. I have been in Miami Beach once, but it was in 1958, and on this matter also, documented testimony can be provided.

Finally, as to the reference to my lack of military service which I take to be a matter of personal curiosity unrelated to the legal sufferances, I refer you to the records of Selective Service Board 118, Philadelphia, Pa., where you will find one Mason Clark Greer (Selective Service No. 8-165-35-114) classified as IV-F, or Unfit for Military Service, due to a partially punctured eardrum resulting from an unsuccessful attempt at age nine years to fly.

I hope this clarifies all existing confusion and suspicions. If not, I shall be glad to answer any further questions in regard to my book.

All best wishes,

Mason Clark Greer

NOVEMBER 9

FROM QUENTIN L. GRU

Berry, Lock & Gru
Attorneys at Law
1136 Michigan Avenue
Chicago, Illinois

Mr. Guy LaDouche
c/o Mr. Mason Greer
P.O. Box 15
Camphor, Vermont

November 7

Re: Dibbs vs. LaDouche a/k/a Greer
a/k/a Chernow

Dear Mr. LaDouche:

Our client, Lt. Commander E. B. Dibbs, has today turned over to me your letter of November 3 to him. In my capacity as his attorney, I have advised Lt. Commander Dibbs that this letter may well constitute additional grounds for a defamation action against you. I feel certain that if you contact your attorney, he will advise you, for your own protection, to cease communication with Lt. Commander Dibbs.

As of this date, I have received no message from you or your attorney acknowledging receipt of the complaint sent to you on November 1. In the event you did not receive that complaint, I am enclosing herewith a new copy as well as a carbon of my covering letter and a copy of a second complaint. You will notice that this second complaint is identical in all respects to the first, with the exception of the amount of damages being requested and a change in the alias of the defamer.

I am hopeful of hearing from you or your attorney concerning this matter in the near future.

Yours truly,

Quentin L. Gru

QLG:cj
Encs.
cc: Lt. Commander E. B. Dibbs

NOVEMBER 10

FROM DAVID NOODLEMAN, MIAMI, FLORIDA

Thursday

Dear Mase,

What gives? We haven't heard from you since about August when you said you were sending us a bunch of love letters and all we got was an envelope full of sand. If that's a joke, I don't get it. In fact I don't understand half the things you write. We had a writer from *Skyways* in the shop last week to do an article on us called "Inside Reliable Propeller Service." If they ever make a movie out of it, I'll try to swing the job your way.

Who have you been making lately? I wish to hell you'd send me the names of your scores because they could just pop up down here. A million college gash were in town this summer but I was so up to my wazoo in work I hardly got a look at them. But I had a new secretary for two weeks (#135!), Janet Vallenti. Huge boobs. But now Mrs. Seidlap is back.

Eddie Scornamie came in to see me the other day. He opened a pizza place over on the beach but the racket boys ran him out and killed his brother. He says he's broke and tried to hit me for a grand. He's been in town for 3 mos. and never gave me a ring before. You don't know who your friends are until they're in trouble.

Do you ever hear from Mitch? Monty stopped by here from Denver on his way to Hawaii for a few months. I wish I was his travel agent. I remember when he met us in New York from Atlanta on his way to San Francisco. I guess he can't spend that dough fast enough before the new stack rolls in. It's like I've always said. It's not who you are but who you're born that counts. Personally, if I had his dough, I'd buy up Elizabeth Taylor and her house and keep Cora on as the maid. You can have Sophia Loren for my money. All those Italian girls play around on the side.

Write me and fill me in on all the news. Everybody here sends love.

Your bazoom buddy,

Dave

NOVEMBER 12

FROM BENJAMIN WINK

November 10

Dear Mase—Just a note in answer to yours of November 6 and to send you the enclosed clipping. I made a Thermofax of it for Kenny but thought you might want the original. If you think I'm the only one who takes special notice of you, boy, just read this. Guess you're well into the new one by now. I cant wait to see it. I've been going crazy trying to find something to read at nights. Last week I took all your old books down from the shelf and read them straight through again. You've got it, Mase, boy, the stuff all the great ones had. I can hardly stand to read Kenny's books the first time. I told him about your idea to do another book on f - - - - - - - m, but he said, "Only a hack repeats himself." "Mase repeats himself sometimes," I said. "I rest my case," he said. Well, the royalty figures show who's the hack in my book. Do you have a title for the new one yet? Art suggested *Voodoo Virgin* if the book has anything to do with voodoo. I mentioned your idea about Dickens being Shakespeare to the professor who does those *Increase Your Brain Power* books for us. He said that Shakespeare died 200 years before Dickens was born. Did you know that? If it's true, you'll have to get around it somewhere in the book. But if anyone can do it, you can. Keep blasting, fella!

Ben

ENCLOSURE FROM BENJAMIN WINK,
CLIPPING FROM THE *WILKINS COMMERCIAL*,
WILKINS, MD.

found in his room were 114 volumes of paperbound pornography. Beneath such titles as "Orgy Girl," "These Raging Loins," "Sin for Your Supper" and "Touch Me, Touch Me," blazed illustrations of partially denuded girls in poses describing terror, pleasure or acquiescence. The back covers synopsized the stories in provocative ways, as in the case of "Brothers-in-Lust," published by Scepter Books and authored by Guy LaDouche:

"Sexperts or Perverts? The lusts of the Slade Brothers knew no bounds.... There was Tom Slade, big, blond and handsome, who sold bis body to the highest bidder... Dick Slade, with a strange glint in his eye that became even stranger when there was a razor in his hand.... And Harry Slade, young and innocent, until a girl of the streets taught him the most depraved tricks of the trade."

Another Scepter Book, "Of Beastly Lust," showed a man, a naked girl and a seal-like animal in the darkness of a barn. "Strange Desires Filled His Sin-Crazed Mind," read the cover.

Bimmler, who lived in the next room, said Spragg often bought as many as five such books each day and boasted that

NOVEMBER 13

FROM LT. COMMANDER E. B. DIBBS

10 November

February, 1957?
Squaw Valley, California?
Ski instruction?

Sound familiar to you, my dear Vechtenmeisser?

I warned you that it was only a matter of time before my daughter recalled you. When we finally meet, neither your infamous charm nor your Hapsburg relations will be of any protection. However, since you choose to pose as a nobleman, I have instructed my attorneys to increase the damages to $300,000.

As regards your impudent letter of 8 November, I have taken steps to verify the Selective Service information pertaining to Mason Clark Greer. If this information proves correct, I will inform the Federal Bureau of Investigation and a search for Mr. Greer will be instigated.

My attorneys are enlightened as to these new developments and you shall be hearing from them shortly.

Yours truly,

*Lt. Commander E. B. Dibbs, USN
(Ret.)*

TO LT. COMMANDER E. B. DIBBS

Nov 13

Dear Poison Pen Pals:

I am in receipt of your letter of Nov 10 as well as Gru's letter of Nov 7 enclosing a second complaint and a copy of the first complaint and a carbon of his letter of Nov 1.

I think that shows I'm a good sport. I would now like to ask you to let the gag drop. You had me going for a while in round two, with the Gru letter, but you killed it with your Hapsburg ski instructor and Dave's untimely note. If perchance you're not Dave and Monty I no longer care who you are. I am repentant enough that I have acquaintances so ill-humored.

In any case, I am dropping the bit from this end and you can expect no further replies from me. However, your continued sozzle in the sty of your humor can still create discomfort for me. You see, I live sixteen winding, hazardous miles from the village. It is not a pleasant drive even in the best weather, and now that it's started to snow, every time I go out my good ear begins to ring. So I don't go out except when it's absolutely necessary. To that purpose I have contrived an arrangement with the postmaster who hoists a red flag to a height visible from my cabin whenever there is mail for me. Five times in the past week that flag has gone up and I have come down to find only Dibbs-Gru nonsense. If you are not moved by my agonies, consider with pity the chapped hands of the postmaster.

I am sending a carbon of this to your fellow conspirator, Gru, to help put a stop to this merry-go-round. It has been good fun; I appreciate your efforts to amuse the hermit and I am not unreasonably angry. But I have a deadline coming at me on ice skates. In effect, you two are standing between

30,000 haggard high school boys and the bathroom. Get
out of the way!

Madly,
Ferdinand D. Butt

TO QUENTTN L. GRU

Mr. Quentin L. Gru
Berry, Lock & Gru
1136 Michigan Avenue
Chicago, Illinois

November 13

Re: Nonsense

Dear Mr. Gru:
The enclosed carbon speaks for itself and may be considered my reply to your two previous letters and any which may now be in transit. Any further correspondence received from you shall be returned to you, C.O.D., in a box containing many heavy, useless objects.

If you really are a lawyer, you must be very unsuccessful to have so much time for foolishness.

Yours truly,
Mason C. Greer

TO BENJAMIN WINK

Nov 13

Dear Ben:

Thanks for your note of Nov 10 and the clipping which caught my curiosity. What did my ardent fan, Spragg, do to warrant such coverage? If you have the complete clipping, I'd appreciate a copy.

Unusual circumstances have prevented me from starting the new book as yet but I'm going to get on it first thing tomorrow. It should be to you in plenty of time for the December run. Thank Art for *Voodoo Virgin,* which is indeed a natural, but not for me. My religious background is too limited. The best I could manage would be *Presbyterian Hellcat* which I think lacks pow. Why don't you throw the *Voodoo* plum to Kenny?

All best,

Mase

NOVEMBER 14

FROM THOMAS O. LOCK

Berry, Lock & Gru
Attorneys at Law
1136 Michigan Avenue
Chicago, Illinois

Mr. Karl Vechtenmeisser
c/o Mr. Mason Greer
P.O. Box 15
Camphor, Vermont

November 10

Re: Dibbs vs: LaDouche a/k/a Greer
a/k/a Vechtenmeisser

Dear Mr. Vechtenmeisser:

In light of recent complications enumerated by our client, Lt. Commander E. B. Dibbs, in his letter to you of November 10,1 have replaced my colleague, Mr. Gru, as chief counsel for Lt. Commander Dibbs and his daughter, Barbara Victoria. It would greatly facilitate matters if you would address all future correspondence to me rather than to Mr. Gru.

Reviewing Mr. Gru's file on this case, I find no record, as of this date, of any reply by you or your attorney to this office. Nonetheless, in your letter of November 8 to Lt. Commander Dibbs, you acknowledged receipt of Mr. Gru's letter of November 1 and the enclosed complaint. In the event you did not receive Mr. Gru's letter of November 7 and the enclosures, I am enclosing here with a carbon of that letter and a copy of that complaint. In addition, I am enclosing herewith a copy of a new complaint. You will notice that this complaint is identical in all respects to the previous two with the exception of the amount of damages being requested and a change in the alias of the defamer.

In his letter of November 7, Mr. Gru advised you, for your own protection, to secure legal representation and cease communicating with Lt. Commander Dibbs. I would like to strongly reiterate this advice. We have also advised our clients to cease communicating with you.

I am hopeful of hearing from you or your attorney concerning this matter in the near future.

Yours truly,

Thomas O. Lock

TOL:cj
Encs.
cc: Lt. Commander E. B. Dibbs

NOVEMBER 17

FROM LT. COMMANDER E. B. DIBBS

15 November

So the rat is beginning to panic?

Well, perhaps you will be incited to greater frenzy to learn that today I have posted a letter to my close friend, General George U. Pfaff, USA (Ret.), requesting him to initiate a complete inquiry into your background, immigration and, particularly, your allegiances and whereabouts during the periods 1914–1918 and 1933–1945. If these findings are as I suspect, I will have the great pleasure of facing you in a Court of International Justice in the near future.

Yours truly,

> *Lt. Commander E. B. Dibbs, USN*
> *(Ret.)*

P.S. I would appreciate it if you make no mention of our correspondence to my attorneys.

> *E. B. D.*

TO LT. COMMANDER E. B. DIBBS,
SPECIAL DELIVERY

Nov 17

Dear Sir:

Upon receipt of your letter of Nov 15, I reviewed our entire correspondence from its inception and my related correspondence with your attorneys, Messrs. Berry, Lock and Gru. This survey revealed to me a startling fact which had escaped my notice during piecemeal scannings. Consequently, I am taking this opportunity to present anew my analysis of this entire matter.

I no longer suspect you to be a fictitious personality created by friends for the purpose of my harassment. I now know you to be a real person who is either a crank, a lunatic or a grotesquely original combination of these aberrations.

I am speeding this letter to you at great Special Delivery expense in order that you may receive it in advance of the Thanksgiving Holiday. I feel it fitting, at this time of national gratitude, and in accordance with your avowed duty to your country (if you are a retired naval officer), that you surrender yourself to the care of the nearest physician, law enforcement agent or responsible citizen. You are dangerously ill, sir. Your mind has loosed itself from any moorings in reality and is bobbing perilously in seas of fantasy. You are a potential threat to your own well-being and an annoyance to any person with the poor luck to come in contact with you. Explain this to your capturer and ask him to convey you to the nearest hospital, clinic or sanitarium. Do this now; do not dally.

It is my personal although unsubstantiated opinion that your daughter should accompany you and file voluntary papers of her own if this institution also treats nymphomaniacal personalities. All best wishes,

Mason C. Greer

cc: Sacasas, Illinois, Police Department
    Illinois State Highway Patrol
    Illinois State Hospital for the Criminally Insane
    Pentagon (Retired Officers Division)

NOVEMBER 19

FROM THOMAS O. LOCK

Berry, Lock & Gru
Attorneys at Law
1136 Michigan Avenue
Chicago, Illinois

Mr. Karl Vechtenmeisser
c/o Mr. Mason Greer
P.O. Box 15
Camphor, Vermont

November 16

Re: Dibbs vs. LaDouche a/k/a Greer
a/k/a Vechtenmeisser
a/k/a Bull

Dear Mr. Vechtenmeisser:
   I am in receipt of your letter of November 13 to Mr. Gru and the enclosed carbon of your letter of that date to Lt. Commander Dibbs. Both of these correspondences seem to be slightly incoherent and in avoidance of the matter at hand. Again I would urge you to seek legal counsel and abandon this attempt at self-representation.
   The legal profession is a complicated one, Mr. Vechtenmeisser, and the best interests of justice are not served when the presentation of either side of a case is handled by the inexperienced or uninformed. If it is a matter of finances which is preventing you from seeking professional counsel, I would suggest contacting the Legal Aid Society or Public

Defender's Office. I have taken the liberty of enclosing herewith listings of both of these organizations.

However, should you insist upon representing yourself, I am moved by a spirit of "fair play" to intimate that you consult 133 Ill. 474 (Overfelder vs. Thrump), a defamation suit very similar in all pertinent aspects to this one. In that instance you will note that the damages awarded the defamed party exceeded $800,000.

I am hopeful of hearing from you or your attorney in the near future.

Yours truly,

Thomas O. Lock

TOL:cj
Encs.
cc: Lt. Commander E. B. Dibbs

NOVEMBER 20

TO THOMAS LOCK,
COVER LETTER TO PARCEL

Nov 20

Mr. Lock:
   I hope you will find the enclosed useful.
   All best wishes for a happy holiday season.
   Yours truly,

Mason C. LaDouche

NOVEMBER 21

FROM LT. COMMANDER E. B. DIBBS

19 November

The oppressor calls his victims insane! An old Nazi trick, Vechtenmeisser. I had expected better of you.

I have shown your letter to my close friend, Dr. Pietro Quinones, well-known psychoanalyst and author of the book *The Petulant Child: A Psychiatric Biography of Himmler.* He was highly amused by your attempt to plant indications of a hallucinatory personality in order to fall back on an insanity plea. He thought your little trick of addressing me as if I were several persons was clever enough to fool most of the psychiatrists in this country. I applaud your cunning. Unfortunately for you, Dr. Quinones has agreed to testify as alienist at your trial.

Why don't you have a telephone or obtainable home address, Karl? Frightened? You cannot hide in a post office box forever. When you come out, waiting for you shall be,

Lt. Commander E. B. Dibbs, USN
(Ret.)

FROM BENJAMIN WINK,
COVER LETTER TO PARCEL

November 19

Dear Mase—Just a note to answer yours and to send along a copy of Bill's latest, *Early to Bed*. Thought you might like to see how far behind the competition is. How's the new one coming? Art is dying to get his hands on it so he can start work on the cover. We are dropping the *Voodoo* idea on the shelf for a while as Kenny doesn't want it either, but Art has a great idea for a new cover showing two Negresses and this one white fella walking into a bedroom together. Is there any chance of a scene like that being in your book? If so, drop me a line and I'll get Art started on it. Sorry to say I don't have a copy of the clipping you asked for. It came the way I sent it. Are there any others you want? You know we get three papers every day right here in the office. Art just reminded me that somebody from the F.B.I. was in asking for you. Art thought it was a raid and locked himself in the storeroom with all the new stuff. But it was only a joke, thank God. Somebody reported you as dead. "Dead?" I said. You're the livest thing on the market. It might have been Kenny. Let me know about Art's idea as soon as you can. Any title yet? Sorry again about the clipping. Keep your guard up, fella! And a Happy Thanksgiving!

Ben

NOVEMBER 22

TO MICHAEL WESTLAKE,
C/O TARGUM, RHODES,
MEERS & MEADOWS, ATTORNEY AT LAW,
NEW YORK CITY,
COVER LETTER TO PARCEL

Nov 22

Dear Mitch:

I'm sorry to bother you with a letter, especially since you've been considerate enough not to bother me with one for eight months. I know part of the reason is that you still haven't forgiven me for becoming Required Reading for every lecher, pervert and spinster in America. But I think another part is that you've been too busy making sure small businesses like General Motors aren't being stifled by paying corporate income tax.

Well, it was all down there in the Marie Edsington Fish H. S. Yearbook, if you recall. (Writing is Mase Greer's forte / We're sure to hear of him someday.) (Remember Michael Westlake's name / He may put Clarence Darrow to shame.) Who would have ever thought, eh? Maybe we never had a hope of doing any better. The only one I know who really seems to be approaching his life's goal is Dave. At last report he had notched #135, although personally I think 130 of them have been Cora in different nightgowns. And poor Monty, whose meager ambition is to die in a plane crash on Mt. Calvary while drinking champagne on his 33rd birthday, has about ten months to make it or he might as well shoot himself. I've been out of touch with the others but the last I heard Ernie hadn't found a cure for cancer and I don't believe Fred is President of the United States.

So I can forgive your trespasses if you can forgive mine. And at least I've been considerate enough not to pass on my futile seed by spawning heirs. How are the heirs, by the way? If you don't send old Godfather a picture, old Godfather will send them one of his books.

I'm sending you one in this package. No American bathroom should be without a copy, but in this case it's for business first. The enclosed papers will explain the situation more clearly than I could. I've arranged them in the order in which I received or mailed them since the dates they were written make things somewhat confusing. This Berry, Lock & Gru outfit seems to operate in a time zone all their own.

My replies (the urine-yellow sheets) are all re-creations of the originals since I didn't keep carbons. I think they're fairly accurate in tone and content but some of the phrases may be different. In my first letter to Dibbs, I might have called him an old cocker rather than bastard, etc. I was pretty sure he was Dave and Monty then, and diplomacy didn't seem to matter. I'm not sure it does now because if he's real, he's obviously insane.

That's one of the things I'd like you to check for me. You'll understand this better once you've waded through the papers. I've tried to find out if there is an E. B. Dibbs in Sacasas, Ill., but there's no listing. Berry, Lock & Gru, however, as foolish as it sounds, are real. But Lock and Gru have been out every time I've called and nobody's seen Berry since the Peaches Browning scandal. I'm afraid that's as much as I can do from up here and in another few weeks I may be so snowbound that even getting to a phone will be difficult.

Oh yeah. Before I wrote that Thanksgiving note to Dibbs, I called Dave who swore up and down he doesn't know a thing about this. Monty's been in Hawaii since October so I didn't bother to check with him but Dave said he didn't think Monty was in on it either. I don't know of anyone else—except maybe you—who'd have the brattish sense of humor to disrupt my quiet life.

That's what made me first think this might be on the

level. Since then a few pieces have fallen into place, last of all the F.B.I., mentioned in the last note from Wink, my editor. Also there is a Dr. Pietro Quinones, who is a psychoanalyst and author. I read his book on Himmler. He is probably a friend of Dibbs, too, because that book was the work of another madman. He traced Himmler's adult actions back to their childhood causes and came up with the astonishing computation that every time baby Heinrich was allowed to suck his thumb, 200 Jews were sentenced to death. That's a lot of thumbsucking and so is the rest of the book.

In any case, if this suit is legit, naturally I'd like you to handle my defense. It could be the chance of a lifetime for you. You might get in touch with the lawyer for Scepter as I imagine they'll be named codefendants. But the first thing I'd like you to do is call Berry, Lock & Gru before they put me on the relief rolls. Have them correspond with you from now on. My cabin is very small and until I decided to make you my savior, I was ass-deep in their complaints.

Which reminds me. The only scrap of garbage related to this mess which I'm not enclosing is the listings of Public Defenders and Legal Aid Societies B. L. & G. sent me. As promised, I dispatched it back to them, C.O.D., in a package containing thirty pounds of Vermont rock. As soon as I left the post office, I realized how this thing was getting to me, then came Wink's last letter and I decided I'd best seek your help.

It's four-thirty in the afternoon now. I've spent my whole Thanksgiving Day assorting and writing this garbage. The sky is getting dark and I think I see snow clouds gathering around the mountains. I generally hate snow but if it will fall in sufficient quantity to keep me from my mail and another letter from Lt. Commander E. B. Dibbs, USN (Ret), I will carry a little wet ball of it in my pocket forever.

Don't fail me on this, Mitch. Love to Marge and the brood.

Edmond Dantes,
the Count of Monte Cristo

NOVEMBER 23

FROM MISS NATALIE BONKERS,
NORTH HIGHLAND, N.J.

Tuesday night

Dear Mase,

After writing two letters to you and not getting any answer, I had almost given up hope of ever hearing from you again. Now that you've finally done me the honor of replying, I almost wish you hadn't. I certainly wish you had written to me directly instead of to Mr. Janosslit. When he showed me your letter, I thought at first it was serious and didn't connect it with you at all. It didn't seem like your style of writing, but then I have no idea how you write when you're doing something serious. Then I began to think about the name you signed, Dibbs, and I remembered it was the name of one of the characters in one of your terrible books. I'm certainly flattered that you knew I'd remember. Me, with my sensational memory. Or were you just flattering yourself by assuming that I couldn't possibly forget one word in any book *you* wrote?

I'm trying to give you the benefit of every doubt and say that your letter was just a joke and not meant to be cruel or humiliating. But you must know that not everyone shares your sense of humor. I do, I think, but S.E.S. is not the least bit liberal and Mr. Janosslit is a very old-fashioned principal.

There was absolutely nothing I could say in defense of your letter so I just kept quiet and let Mr. Janosslit and Mrs. Haas, the Dean of Girls, lecture me. As you can imagine it was awfully humiliating. Finally Mr. Janosslit said he was going to forget about the incident because of my perfect attendance record. But he's keeping the letter for my permanent file. So, like it or not, a part of you will be with me now wherever I go. I wonder if you thought about that when you wrote it.

To be perfectly honest with you, I think you were acting like that boy I told you about who went around lying to all of his friends about what he and I did together. That's a terribly adolescent attitude, Mase. Especially for someone who writes the kind of books you do and should really have a more sophisticated view of such things. I know you'll think it's funny that I should talk about sophistication. I know I'm not nearly as modern about some things as you are, but I can't help the way I was raised. After the bus left I did have the urge to get off at the first stop and go running back to you. But now I don't regret not doing it. I guess I'm just not the woodnymph type. But I did enjoy our times together and I'm sorry if you didn't and picked that letter as your way of telling me.

If you want to write again, I'd love to hear from you. But please, please write to me directly next time. Even if you don't write, I know I'll never forget you and I hope you won't forget me right away.

Always,
Natalie

FROM DAVID NOODLEMAN, MIAMI, FLORIDA

Wednesday

Dear Mase,
    Ever since you called Friday Cora and I have been sitting up nights trying to figure what it was all about. I don't mind sitting up nights, but not with Cora. What gives? You talked so fast and half the time Cora was mouthing off on the extension that all I got was something about a Navy Commodore. If the draft is bugging you, I know a few people. Last month we did a rush on a Navy plane for this Col. Yapes who was in a big sweat to get down to his shack job in Venezuela. He uses the same toilet as Hockstader when he's in Washington so maybe he can do something. I thought your bum ear was keeping you out. If not, maybe my asthma and three kids isn't going to do me any good.
    We got a card from Monty that had his hotel on it but Nancy ate it. I think it was a Hilton. How many first class hotels can they have on Hawaii? But I don't know how much good Monty can do you because the gov't. is still sore at him about that camp he built them that sank. I tried calling you to find out the poop on this but the operator wouldn't give me your unlisted number, even when I told her it was an emergency. I don't know how somebody's going to reach you in a real emergency. You better talk to her.
    Everything else is fine but business is lousy. Cora's sister is staying with us for a while, but since that time in New York she don't know who I am. When are you coming down again? We're adding on two new rooms so there's plenty of space. If Cora's sister stays on you won't have to leave the house for anything.
    Cora read one of your new books. *Passion Something.* She thought it was great but she likes anything dirty. I thought it was okay but just like all the others. Cora's sister

is reading it now and maybe it will warm her up a little. Norman recognized your picture in my office the other day but he thought your name was Jerry. He wants to read your book now too, but Cora says he's too young. I say they're never too young.

This is turning into a book too. Maybe you could add a couple of grabs and sell it for me. Did I ever tell you that I wanted to be a writer once? I wouldn't have to make up my ideas either, just my life story. I'd call it *The Tan Tornado*.

I met a guy on the in who says don't bet the Redskins this week. Nottenkamper's arm is gone.

Call me and let me in on this draft stuff. Maybe we can pay off Cora's brother to go in instead. Everybody here sends love.

Dave

NOVEMBER 24

FROM DR. PIETRO QUINONES,
OSAK MEDICAL BUILDING, SACASAS, ILL.

November 21

Dear Mr. Vechtenmeisser:
I have taken the liberty of obtaining your address from
Lt. Commander E. B. Dibbs and I write to you in the interest
of Science and the betterment of Mankind.

Great scientific and medical contributions have been
made by outcasts, degenerates and criminals who have
volunteered themselves as subjects for research. I cite the
numerous convicts who have offered themselves as test cases
in the study of cancer, malaria and artificial insemination.
Although these men reap no individual reward for their
efforts, they go to their deaths happier in the knowledge
that they have finally made some contribution to Society.

I call on you now, before the wheels of Justice begin to
grind and crush and embitter your spirit, to aid me in such
an unselfish scientific endeavor.

Perhaps, as a fellow author, you are familiar with my book,
The Petulant Child: A Psychiatric Biography of Himmler
(Dambroke & Neurstag, $5.95). I am presently at work on
a companion volume, *The Fanciful Child: A Psychiatric
Study of Pornographers.* It is for this project that I solicit
your help. Although it would be ideal if you could come to
Sacasas and put yourself under my personal surveillance, I
can understand, in the light of your impending trial and
imprisonment, why you might be unwilling to do this. As
an alternative, I propose a study by correspondence and
enclose a primary questionnaire and self-administrable test
for you to complete and return to me. All information will

be kept in the strictest secrecy and used only for professional purposes. Should your case appear in my book, you will be referred to only as Subject V.

It is not often that one has the chance to make a contribution to generations yet unborn. I hope you will not let your opportunity pass unfulfilled. A stamped, self-addressed envelope is also enclosed.

Looking forward to hearing from you soon, I remain,

Sincerely yours,
Dr. Pietro Quinones

ENCLOSURE FROM DR. QUTNONES

I. ANSWER THE FOLLOWING QUESTIONS AS COMPLETELY AS
POSSIBLE:
A. NAME: _____
B. DATE OF BIRTH: _____
C. PLACE OF BIRTH: _____

II. ANSWER THE FOLLOWING QUESTIONS BY CIRCLING THE
APPROPRIATE LETTER:
A. SEX: M   F   H
B. COLOR: W B Y R OTHER (IF OTHER, INDICATE
HERE _____)
C. MARITAL STATUS: S   M   D   W

III. ANSWER THE FOLLOWING QUESTIONS BRIEFLY BUT
COMPLETELY:
A. HOW LONG HAVE YOU BEEN WRITING PORNOGRAPHY?
_____
_____

B. DESCRIBE THE FIRST PIECE OF PORNOGRAPHY YOU
WROTE: _____
_____

C. WHY DO YOU FEEL YOU WROTE IT? _____
_____

D. WRITE AS MUCH OF IT AS YOU CAN REMEMBER. (USE
SEPARATE SHEET IF NECESSARY, OR ENCLOSE COPY OF
PIECE IF POSSIBLE) _____
_____

E. WHAT WAS YOUR AGE WHEN YOU WROTE THIS PIECE
OF PORNOGRAPHY? _____
_____

F. DID YOU SHOW IT TO ANYONE? IF SO, HOW? _____
_____

G. WHAT WAS YOUR OPINION OF THIS PIECE OF PORNOGRAPHY AT THE TIME YOU WROTE IT? _____

_____

H. WHAT IS YOUR OPINION OF THIS PIECE OF PORNOGRAPHY NOW ? _____

_____

I. WHAT CHANGES WOULD YOU MAKE IN IT NOW?_____

_____

J. HOW LONG WAS IT AFTER YOU COMPLETED THIS PIECE OF PORNOGRAPHY UNTIL YOU ENGAGED IN SEXUAL INTERCOURSE? _____

_____

K. WHAT TYPE OF SEXUAL INTERCOURSE DID YOU ENGAGE IN? _____

_____

L. IN WHAT WAY WAS THE PORNOGRAPHIC WORK RELATED TO THAT ACT OF SEXUAL INTERCOURSE? _____

_____

IV. FILL IN THE BLANKS IN THE FOLLOWING SENTENCES WITH THE FIRST WORD OR WORDS THAT COME TO MIND.
   A. MY FAVORITE PART OF THE BODY IS THE _____
   B. THREE THINGS I LIKE TO DO WITH THIS PART ARE _____ AND _____ AND _____
   C. MY PRIVATE NAME FOR THIS PART IS _____

V. ANSWER THE FOLLOWING QUESTIONS BRIEFLY BUT COMPLETELY:
   A. DESCRIBE THE MOST RECENT PIECE OF PORNOGRAPHY YOU WROTE: _____

   _____

   B. WHY DO YOU FEEL YOU WROTE IT? _____

   _____

   C. WRITE AS MUCH OF IT AS YOU CAN REMEMBER. (USE SEPARATE SHEET IF NECESSARY OR ENCLOSE COPY OF PIECE IF POSSIBLE) _____

   _____

D. What was your age when you wrote this piece of pornography? _____

_____

E. Did you show it to anyone? If so, how? _____

_____

_____

F. What was your opinion of this piece of pornography at the time you wrote it? _____

_____

G. What is your opinion of this piece of pornography now? _____

_____

H. What changes would you make in it now? _____

_____

I. How long was it after you completed this piece of pornography until you engaged in sexual intercourse? _____

_____

J. What type of sexual intercourse did you engage in? _____

_____

K. In what way was the pornography work related to that act of sexual intercourse? _____

_____

VI. By drawing lines, connect the words in the following columns in the way which seems most logical to you:

Mother	Fork
Bed	Sister
Father	Black
Body	Brother
White	Head
Knife	Pillow

VII. BELOW ARE THE FIRST SENTENCES OF THREE DIFFERENT STORIES. ON A SEPARATE SHEET OF PAPER, WRITE EACH OF THESE SENTENCES AND THEN COMPLETE THE STORIES IN ANY MANNER YOU WISH.

A. A YOUNG MAN WALKED INTO A PHARMACY. HE WAITED UNTIL ALL THE OTHER CUSTOMERS HAD LEFT. THEN HE APPROACHED THE WOMAN BEHIND THE COUNTER.

B. A MAN AND A WOMAN ARE IN BED TOGETHER. THEY ARE BOTH DISTURBED ABOUT SOMETHING.

C. TWO BOYS ARE PLAYING IN A DARK CELLAR.

NOVEMBER 26

FROM LT. COMMANDER E. B. DIBBS

24 November

Almost a week has passed without a letter from
Vechtenmeisser. Does he stay silent and shivering like a
U-boat? Has he turned tail and run for home like the crippled
Klagmacht? Has he decided to escape justice by turning his
guns on himself like the scurrilous Prince Waldestein?

If you are still alive, Vechtenmeisser, listen to me. Don't
be afraid to write. Where is the spirit of your Aryan
forefathers? Your Hapsburg heritage? Come, let us have one
final encounter before the sword of righteousness runs you
through.

As ever,

Lt. Commander E. B. Dibbs, USN
(Ret.)

NOVEMBER 27

FROM MICHAEL WESTLAKE

November 25

Dear Frank Harris:

I haven't written because I thought you were still living fifteen blocks from the office. Marge, who is suspiciously conscientious about keeping your memory fresh in our house, has suggested almost weekly that I call you to get together over lunch. I have as conscientiously demurred. I remember only too well our last lunch when you told Targum if he really wanted to consider himself a lawyer, he should devote his life to getting a reversal on the Sacco-Vanzetti case. But I have called your old number a few times and either you failed to have it disconnected or the new party is a globetrotter because I have yet to get an answer. Next time you decamp for Camphor, let someone know. Then maybe you'll get some mail.

On second thought you have been getting some mail, haven't you? It took me a full afternoon to sift through that dossier and a full day for Sid and me to check out the more vital points. The results are both good and bad and for the fee I can expect from you, I'm not going to sort them out. Here they are in a lump. Pick the ones you like.

There is a real Lt. Commander E. B. (Everett Bisley) Dibbs, USN (Ret.) in Sacasas, Ill. He does have a daughter named Barbara Victoria, known as Bibbsy, and she is suing you for defamation. Her current asking price is $350,000. As far as we can determine Dibbs has no record of insanity; his naval discharge was with highest honors. Sid is trying to wrangle a look at his service folder but that may be tough. Dibbs is sixty-eight years old; his partial incapacitation is

chronic arthritis centered in the left leg for which he has
a full-time nurse and housekeeper named Hannah Sugar. I
tried to speak to him but Mrs. Sugar informed me that he
is under attorney's instructions not to communicate with
anyone about the case. It was B. L. & G., by the way, who
had his number unlisted recently.

I asked to speak to Bibbsy but she wasn't home, nor has
she been, said Mrs. Sugar, for more than six days in the last
four years. "A sweet thing but wild," Mrs. Sugar described
her, explaining that Bibbsy had attended Applegate, Sayers,
Staunton and Martha Phillips—without ever achieving
sophomore status. She also appeared briefly in the film
Brandy Snifter Goes Wild, a movie that had limited but
selective distribution; in it she wore little except a mask.
Since then, according to Mother Sugar, she has settled down
some and now mostly travels as a kind of stewardess for
the jet set. She was engaged twice, once to whats-his-name,
the Peruvian playboy, but that fell through when neither of
them showed up for the ceremony.

I did get to talk to Lock at B. L. & G. and he was very
happy to hear from me. They are very anxious to settle
out of court, but not for less than $250,000. They believe
they have an air-tight case and the only thing they seemed
worried about is Dibbs running wild enough in his letters to
you to give us some sort of a countersuit. That's an intriguing
notion, but libel demands that the defamatory statements be
seen by a third party in a position to harm the defendant.
I'll leave it to you to work out the details.

Not that their case is air-tight by any means. As a matter
of fact, as far as libel law goes, they don't know their ass
from a barrel full of torts. I don't think they've considered
bringing in Bathroom Books as codefendants and Overfelder
vs. Thrump is a completely invalid precedent. I looked up
the case for the details although I remembered most of it
from school. It was one of those oddball ones that always
came up on exams. I'll bore you with the basic facts just for
laughs. Maybe you can use it in a book sometime.

* * *

Thrump was the owner-editor of the kind of small-town newspaper that prints gossip as a fact and fact as gossip. One day he ran an article alleging that the City Council meeting had been disrupted by the appearance of one Oren Overfelder, local inebriate, who was found sleeping under the mayor's desk. Upon awakening, Overfelder proceeded to roundly curse his persecutors and violate the City Charter. He was finally thrown out, which had happened to him many times before. All this is apparently true. At least when Overfelder saw the article the following day he laughed and admitted it. But his wife was more protective of his good name. She went to Thrump at his home and demanded a retraction and damages. Thrump refused to do either and when he tried to leave to go to his office, Mrs. Overfelder obstinately stood in front of his car which was parked in the driveway. Thrump warned her to get out of the way but she refused and he went inside to call the police. When he came out, he didn't see her so he got in his car and drove off. Right over her. She had been squatting in front of the grille. She suffered a concussion, broken arm, lacerations of the face and shoulders and the loss of twelve teeth. On her behalf, Overfelder sued Thrump for damages to his wife and, on her insistence, threw in the libel charge too. Thrump's lawyer knew they could beat the libel rap but was worried about the assault charge; Overfelder's lawyer knew they were solid on the assault but figured the libel issue might cost them the whole case. The two got together and agreed that Thrump would plead guilty to both charges, not appeal the

huge damages which would be awarded but
that only medical bills and $500 would ever
be paid. Consequently, Thrump was found
guilty, assessed $800,000, paid nothing
because he left town the following day.
Overfelder got drunk and drowned in the city
reservoir the next month and his wife died of
internal complications two weeks after. The
decision was later appealed by Thrump's wife
and reversed for reasons of collusion.

Interesting, no? What it proves, of course, is that we can
wipe up the courtroom with B. L. & G. if they use it. Should
they eventually come up with a case, the worst they could
nick you for would be, say, $25,000. Awards greater than
that are rare in defamation cases unless the libeled party is
well-known. If Dibbs's service record shows that he sunk
a few battleships and some town bigger than Sacasas gave
him a ticker-tape parade, you may be in for a jolt.

If the case does come to court, Toilet Press never heard of
you. I spoke to their lawyer, a Warren Balch, who said they
might consider sponsoring part of your defense provided
there was enough publicity in it and were sure of winning.
He said he'd talk this over with Wink and let me know. At
the moment, they're up to their neck fighting Ladies Clubs
that keep wrecking their presses.

All in all then, I don't think you have too much to worry
about unless Dibbs decides to change lawyers or become
famous. Then we might be in for it. The published disclaimer
in the front of your book is virtually no defense but rather an
effort to discourage potential defamation suits. In this case,
it's going to seem almost facetious. I think you were nuts to
use Bibbsy's real name and description. I can't imagine why
you had anything to do with her in the first place. Charlene
now is another story. She even turns me on. But I hope to
hell there isn't a real Charlene Loffritz floating around.

You know there's an old story which I'm sure you've
heard about what Thomas Wolfe learned from writing

those Asheville books. In paraphrase: It's okay to call a man a horse thief, but you don't have to give his address and phone number. I think the same would apply to whores and nymphomaniacs.

However I am proud that you think I'm competent enough to handle this case. I know if I wanted a book written, I would not go to you. I thought your epic was complete trash, except for Charlene. I get the feeling from your letter that you think so too, and are angling, in your insufferable way, for my absolution. I really don't think my duties as fraternity big brother extend that far. And nobody's absolution is as good as your own. As Targum said, everybody sells out in some way; it's the admission price for living in this less-than-best-possible world. But most people hold something back, too. I only wish we did have G.M. as a client because I firmly believe that they have as much right to justice as the Good Humor man. Law has some highly unsavory aspects, I admit, but by and large I think it's a nice idea and I'm all for it. If what you're doing is pointed in some vaguely wholesome direction, you've got nothing to wring your hands about.

It's now six-thirty in the evening. The sky is black and I think I see rain clouds over the R.C.A. Building. We're having pot roast for dinner tonight. I generally love pot roast but this one will be hard and dry by the time I get to it. I may carry a piece of that hard, dry pot roast in my pocket forever to remind me of all the nice things I do for my friends.

I'll be in touch with you again. Keep Dibbs writing and keep carbons of your replies. Everybody sends regards.

Mitch

NOVEMBER 28

TO LT. COMMANDER E. B. DIBBS

Nov 28

Dear Commander:
It certainly was good to hear from you again. You must excuse my tardiness in not replying sooner but I have been busy with the small Defamation League by which I earn my living. We are not all crochety old water moccasins with our fangs sunk in the thigh of government generosity, you know.

Your last letters, aside from displaying the delirium which has become your trademark, seem to indicate a certain insensate knowledge of the placement of words. Have you ever thought about writing professionally? I feel sure that in the past your demented mind has led you to belabor persons other than myself. Perhaps you would consider compiling those letters in book form. You might call it *Letters from a Crank*. I would be only too pleased to put in a good word with my publisher. Please don't feel that this is any imposition or that your derangement is a handicap in the literary world. In the past alcoholics, epileptics, drug addicts and pederasts have all become successful men of letters. I feel that now the time is eminently right for a first-rate lunatic to burst upon the scene. But you should make haste quickly, sir, for there are many half-cracked writers already at work.

This suggestion does not necessarily preclude my previous one that you and your daughter seek appropriate asylums. After your strenuous career of posing as a naval officer, you might find the solitude of a well-padded room most conducive to writing. But in the broader sense, I feel this would entail a great waste of money and space since your condition appears to be incurable.

But have you given any serious thought to suicide?

How unfortunate that so many useless and mentally infirm citizens do not. If you were of Japanese abstraction (and I have my good friend Admiral Shigoshi Noodlimano of the Imperial Archives checking on that), then I would only have to mention that you are a disgrace to your country and your course of action would be automatic. Likewise, if you were an elder of the Tugarba tribe which inhabits the desert district near Riyadh, Saudi Arabia, you could be given a shovel, dirk and forked stick and you would know your duty. How lamentable that our great country, a whiz in everything technical, has not yet come up with some traditional means for the liquidation of the hopelessly daft such as yourself.

I have given this matter more of my time than you are worth but I believe I have hit upon a fitting disposition. Begin to make a collection of heavy objects such as logs, irons, barbells, rocks. When this collection approaches three hundred pounds, transport it to the nearest body of navigable water. Procure there some sturdy water craft, load your collection of *avoirdupois* on the craft, and steer same to the deepest portion of the water. At this juncture if you have not previously made out your will, you should do so. Then, filling your pockets with as many of the objects as are comfortable, and tightly gripping as many of the others as you feel you can manage, debauch from the boat and enter the water.

Should you feel nostalgic enough about your naval pretensions to wish to maintain them until the end, you might devise some plan of taking the boat down with you. This, however, is optional.

As for your daughter, I feel that the interests of society will not be dangerously hampered if she is permitted to pursue her erotic goals. Being a military poseur, you have, I hope, reminded her that protection starts with p-r-o.

I have received material from your friend, Dr. Quinones, and I can well understand your great kinship. If he is not averse to short sea voyages, why not ask him to accompany you on your little outing? He might use his books as ballast.

I have also been informed that you have contacted Principal Janosslit of Amy Jo Spod Elementary School. Martin Janosslit is my half brother, sir. We have been having sport with you.

Thus far, I have respected your wishes concerning your attorney's knowledge of our protracted correspondence. However, any indication of your disinterest in our correspondence will result in their immediate notification.

All best wishes,

Mason Vechtenmeisser

FROM BENJAMIN WINK

November 26

Dear Mase—Just a note to ask if you got my last couple and Bill's book. Wouldn't want that floating around in the mails. Guess you're right up to the end of the new one by now. If you didn't get my other note, Art has a great idea for a cover. These two Negresses walking into a bedroom with this white fella. I know it's a little riskay but we can see how the first batch moves and if there's any trouble we can always ink down the fella to make it look like three Negroes. It's starting to get good and cold here and does that mean people are going to buy more books or go right home without buying any? I've been in this business one way or another long enough to know you can't tell. Comster thinks we should try some biographies of King Farouk or Porfirio Rubirosa or some movie stars to get a piece of the fan market. But I remember when Larry did a biography of that English actress because they said she was dying, but she didn't; at the same time that other one did, and Wildcat had that biography all ready. I think we should stick to what we know and if they want to throw out money, they should give it to the writers. I don't have to tell you what writers I mean, too. Slam them in the clinches, fella!

Ben

NOVEMBER 29

FROM THOMAS LOCK

Berry, Lock & Gru
Attorneys at Law
1136 Michigan Avenue
Chicago, Illinois

Mr. Karl Vechtenmeisser
c/o Mr. Mason Greer
P.O. Box 15
Camphor, Vermont

November 26

Re: Dibbs vs. LaDouche a/k/a Greer
a/k/a Vechtenmeisser
a/k/a Bull

Dear Mr. Vechtenmeisser:

Your attorney, Mr. Westlake, has been in contact with us and, as he has probably mentioned to you, we are attempting to negotiate a private settlement which will be agreeable to all parties.

Thank you for returning the listings of Legal Aid Societies and Public Defenders' offices. However, this was entirely unnecessary as we have an adequate supply of these directories at our disposal. In any event, I am truly glad you have located an attorney and I am sure you will find that your interests will now be better served than they were previously.

With the above-mentioned listings, however, was a package containing some sort of stones which we assume you mailed to us in error. Since the package was unlabelled as to contents, we had no knowledge of this error at the time of the parcel's arrival. Consequently, the delivery charge of $48.07 was paid by this office and the package was opened. We have no idea of the value of these stones; they appear to be common land stones. In any case, be assured that we are keeping them in our safe pending your instructions, and upon receipt of the above-mentioned charge, we will be glad to ship this carton to its intended destination.

I hope to hear from you regarding this matter in the near future.

Yours truly,

Thomas O. Lock

TOL:cj
cc: Lt. Commander E. B. Dibbs

NOVEMBER 30

TO THOMAS O. LOCK,
COVER LETTER TO PARCEL

Nov 30

Dear Mr. Lock:

Thanks so much for your letter of Nov 26. Naturally I was glad to learn that the rocks arrived intact and that you have them under close observation.

Enclosed please find batch number two. I think it might be wise if these were stored somewhere other than your company safe. Not all our eggs in the same basket, eh?

All best wishes.

Mason C. Dibbs

DECEMBER 1

FROM LT. COMMANDER E. B. DIBBS

29 November

Vechtenmeisser:

You may be disturbed to know that Mason Greer is still alive. Agents of the Federal Bureau of Investigation are currently in search of him. When he is found, the method by which you obtained his Selective Service card will be revealed. The hounds close in on the barbarous wolf.

I have checked my Naval Intelligence maps and can find no listing for a Camphor, Vermont.

Dr. Quinones wishes to know why you will not answer his questionnaire.

As ever.

Dibbs

TO LT. COMMANDER E. B. DIBBS

Dec 1

Dibbs:

Even if you find Greer, he will never testify against me. He is brainwashed.

Camphor, Vermont, is 30 miles from Haute Verde, Vermont, you imbecile. I have had no trouble in locating Sacasas, Illinois. It appears to be conveniently close to the Baynard-Woop Home for the Mentally Indisposed. I suggest you drive there on the next pleasant Sunday and introduce yourself.

If you are in possession of Naval Intelligence maps, they must have been an ironic gift. The donor is no friend of yours. I advise you to take steps to avoid further ridicule. He might next send you a book on figure skating.

Please inform Dr. Quinones that he is not the only quack who has sent me a questionnaire. I will be making my final selection in the next few days. If he is a winner, he shall be notified by mail. Patience is a virtue.

All best.

Wolf Vechtenmeisser

DECEMBER 2

TO MICHAEL WESTLAKE

Dec 2

Dear Jiminy Cricket:
I hope it won't damage your professional standing to defend an innocent man. Everything that disclaimer says is, coincidentally enough, true. I never heard of a Bibbsy Dibbs, any other Bibbsys or Dibbses or anyone with a perfect trapezoidal birthmark on her ass. The same goes for Charlene, unfortunately. They are all figments of my writer's fantasy. I can't explain why my thoughts soar to such bizarre heights but I am thinking of throwing the case to that well-known psychoanalyst and author, Dr. Pietro Quinones. It would be my contribution to unborn bastards. I am serious about this, although I don't expect you to believe me. But I did want you to know I'm not holding anything back.

I came within an ace of losing Dibbs as a pen pal but I think I've charmed him back. The enclosed letters will bring you up to date.

I sent another rock garden to B. L. & G. the other day, in exchange for their last note which is also enclosed. If you don't make them stop writing to me soon, I will no longer be living on a mountain.

Your letter was apparently tampered with en route. Some fanatic typed in a bunch of bullshit about absolution at the bottom. Check your mailman, he may be a Jehovah's Witness. For general information, two thousand kopecks monthly will buy me an unconditional pardon from myself every time. I know that must sound cheap to a lawyer, but you must remember I'm getting in on the ground floor of a growing enterprise. Pornography is definitely on the come.

Now that they've used Henry Miller's glossy pate to batter down the doors of prurience, all the rest of the Club will be pouring in, whips and dirty plumes in hand. Pornographic comics, pornographic children's books (*Leon the Lecherous Lion, Porter the Pederast Porpoise*), pornographic sweatshirts, pornographic beanies, pornographic potties. When we incorporate and get on the big board, you'd be smart to get yourself a piece. In fact, that's our motto.

But I am not in this just for the cash. Money alone cannot compensate a writer for doing a nasty job. It is the work itself that is the great mainstay of the hack because—believe it or not—his love for writing is as great as the artist's. It may even be greater love because the hack usually works more.

Then there is the added satisfaction of attaining one's goal. Granted these books are worthless, but I am not above feeling Ma Barker's cackling pride toward even such disreputable offspring. Sometimes I take one of the books in hand, stare at my cunning pseudonym on the cover, narcissistically stroke the cheap binding. It is a book. I have written it. No one else could have done so in precisely the same way. According to those three precepts, I am akin to Dostoevski, Cervantes, all the greats. Often I riffle the pages and stop to read a line at random. I am in awe that words fill every line and lines fill every page. There are no blank spaces. I have glutted 200 pages with my fictions. And here, in a binding of virgin blush, are 200 more I have done. And 200 more. Three thousand published pages so far. Almost one million words, not many of them forming the same sentences.

Bill Feuer, whose sin pseudonyms include Walter Espanos, Andrew Mark, Brant Hudson and Constance Ball, has papered a wall of his apartment with his book covers. One wall from desk top to ceiling and he has turned the corner. At two books a month for the last three years, he may be the most prolific writer in the world today. He told me once, "They represent achievement. Time, work, creativity. Not everyone could do it."

And as for Selling Down the River on the raft with you and Targum, a writer sells out when he agrees to do a bad book; he consummates the bargain when he knowingly lets a bad book slip from his hands. But during the actual writing, there is no such thing as "selling out" or "writing down." A writer has but one voice and he must use it if he is to write, no matter what he is writing. To try to alter that voice for any sustained period is as difficult as trying to talk in a falsetto for a month. He may simplify, but that is simplification and not easy to do. He may also embellish with prosy curlicues, but that is only obfuscation and the true voice remains beneath the fruity tones. He may revise and rewrite and fill his drawers and trunks and wastebaskets in the process. I prefer to keep my wastebasket empty and fill my wallet, so I publish my little keepsakes.

But make no mistake. They are mine and that is my voice you read. It can't be any other way. The limitations and requirements of the book limit my register and filter my tone like a bad microphone but I am still using my true voice. So if you didn't like *This Flogged Flesh*, the chances are you won't like my "real books" either.

There is even a bright moral side to the picture. I have encountered some ass-brained support for the case that sex books are really goodness and that the maniac who gets his gratification from reading in the bathroom is not likely to hulk rapaciously in the alley. (The glaring exception is, of course, the Spragg case in Wilkins, Md. If you don't know about it, you really should look it up.) There is also evidence that these things are basically moral writings since sinners are usually punished, albeit by other sinners. I know that in my books no one ever screws out of wedlock and survives. Sometimes I have to load them all on a bus and roll it off a cliff to dispose of them, but disposed of they usually are. "Screw and get screwed" is my motto.

And, of course, Art is sufficient justification for anything. If Dostoevski had to bash in a little old woman to get the feel for *Crime and Punishment*, well, isn't that book worth any number of old Russian women? Even Wink says an artist should be allowed to shout from the housetops. I am going up on the roof now and give a little yell.

Recently I received a communique from D. Noodleman of the International Jewish Conspiracy. He did not send regards.

Tell your wife that I love her and shall come for her soon.

The Highwayman

DECEMBER 3

FROM MRS. FRANKLIN GREER, PHILADELPHIA, PA.

Dear Mason,

I hope you have not stopped doing anything important just to read a letter from me. Maybe I will mark Unimportant on the envelope so you will know.

I know you are well because I spoke to Mrs. Westlake yesterday. She has just returned from spending the Thanksgiving holiday with Michael and his family and remarked to me that Michael has been in touch with you some. She said he is your lawyer in a liebel suit against some Army captain because of one of your books. I told her I knew about it and I was not worried because you wrote to me every week. It was one of the longest lies I have ever told.

Is this one of the books that make you so much money but I can never read? Do I know the Army officer in question, by any chance? Mrs. Westlake did not recall his name but she remarked he was elderly and partly crippled. I am thinking about old Captain Reynolds who used to live across from us. I remember you never liked him. Is he the one?

I hope it is not too cold where you are now. We have had a very bad winter so far as you might have read in the newspapers. Uncle Steven and his wife drove in from Boston to spend Thanksgiving Day with me. Celeste called. She remarked that she had not heard from you in several months. I lied again and told her that you were fine. Frank can say a few words now. Frank is your nephew, you may remember.

The Hoopers sold their house and moved down to St. Petersburg, Florida. Is that nearby to David Noodleman? I told them to give him regards. Dr. and Mrs. Ray are moving to California. Mr. Keefe died last week. His wife remarked to me that she thought it was a mercy as he was very sick, but I feel she will come to think differently about it as the years pass. Mrs. Arngren's son had a boy.

I do not know if these things interest you, but if you would like to reply please feel free to do so. In case you have lost my address, it is on the back of this envelope. It has not changed in the last fifteen years, but you have.

My love to you,

Mother

DECEMBER 4

TO MRS. FRANKLIN GREER

Dec 4

Mother?

Mother.

I know I've heard that name before. Didn't they have a special day for you last spring? Flowers and candy and all?

Well, whoever you are, it was nice to hear from you. You shouldn't believe this but I was going to call the day your letter arrived. Two nights ago, I had a dream about the time Mr. Stern, that poor beleaguered old man who ran the only nonprofit candy store in town, gave Mitch and me credit on a pair of those broomhandle pretzel sticks—the ones they stopped making when they found out kids couldn't hurt themselves with them. Well, I had the good sense to gobble down mine before we got home. But conservative, vested-interests old Mitch first licked all the salt off his, then contemplated the bare dough for about two blocks and finally began to nibble cautiously at the edges. Consequently, he still had about two feet of pretzel left when he paraded into his house. He told me about the scene the next day. Violent accusations of theft by his mother; a calm point-by-point rebuttal by Mitch. Loud, dramatic demands for punishment by Mrs. W.; a quiet, humble plea for acquittal by the defendant. An irrevocable verdict of guilty by the judge, his mother, who delayed sentencing long enough to call you and imply that another member of the ring might be hiding on your premises.

You were not one for verbal subtleties then. I see you've changed, too. You grabbed me by a forelock, pried open my mouth, and with one majestic gouge of index finger around gum line, produced a gob of irrefutable, undigested evidence.

At that point I bolted awake because I remembered that the Westlake-Greer Wire Service was still in operation and that the senior partner traditionally crashed the Thanksgiving Dinner given by her son. So I was going to call you and explain this thing before you got the garbled version. I hope I'm still in time for the late city editions.

Mrs. Westlake needs a hearing aid and you need a dictionary. It's not a liebel suit, it's a Bible suit. And he's not an Army captain, he's a barmy chaplain. Some foggy old fogey who's taking issue with a Biblical quotation I used in my last book, *The Cheery Pastor of Cherry Grove*. Of course, he's read the King James version and I used the Douay (the copy dear Reverend Blasfor sold me), so the case will be a draw at best. But Mitch is trying to get him to listen to reason and...

No, huh?

Well, how about this: Mrs. Westlake got the charge right but the people wrong. I'm suing the chaplain, see, for allegations...

I'm suing Mitch?

The chaplain is suing Mitch and I'm on the jury!

Well, anyhow, there's nothing to worry about. Mitch hasn't lost a case since the Great Pretzel Trial. Unfortunately, his mother is going up for the prosecution.

But I'm more concerned about your case. I'm suing you for slander; for telling Mrs. Westlake that I write to you every week. And for defamation of character by telling Celeste that I am fine. The facts are very plain. I am obviously not fine and that's why I haven't written. I am probably the unfinest person you know. I am not even the finest in my finite field any longer because I am finally about to miss a deadline and fine old Mr. Wink may write *fin* to my literary career.

And now, Mother, I know that you want to get into the act. So, as the page girl puts up your card, I reach into the wings for your hand ("Ladies and gentlemen, my Mother!") and you come tripping out in all your ragtag finery.

Mother: It could be the best thing that ever happened to you.

Mason: It will probably be the worst.

Mother: You wont starve.

Mason: That's never been the height of my ambition...
Two, three, four, we cross to the other side of the stage.

Mother: You think you were getting to your ambition by writing those...

Mason: Sex books.

Mother: I don't care how many you wrote. They were trash, all of them.

Mason: How do you know? You didn't read any.... *Back and dip, and now you go around me.*

Mother: You told me so yourself.

Mason: I was being modest. Wink says I'm one of the greats.

Mother: One of the great wastes of talent.

Mason: Let's leave talent out of this, please. I don't tell people you used to dance at Minsky's.

Mother: Irving said I was one of the greats.

Mason: Why didn't you go on with it?

Mother: I met your father. We got married.

Mason: I met money. We're engaged.... *Smile and bow.*

Mother: How much money does it take to make you unhappy?

Mason: Two thousand dollars for a month's wor— Hold it. You changed that line.

Mother: I'm surprised you're still smart enough to realize it. A few more months of garbage for imbeciles and you'll be one yourself.

Mason: A garbage or an imbecile? Watch your antecedent.

Mother: Is she in the audience?

Mason: *Pause for laugh, now promenade.*

Mother: What if you were meant to be a real writer?

Mason: Then I will be.

Mother: Nobody gets to be a writer without writing. You think you can make a book out of the air?

Mason: I'm writing.

Mother: Garbage.

Mason: It's training.... Go *into your spin.*

Mother: Training to write more garbage.

Mason: I'm apprenticing myself to the craft.

Mother: A twenty-eight-year-old apprentice.

Mason: Some of the greatest writers never wrote a word until they were fifty.

Mother: And what about that Irish boy who made such a success at twenty-four?

Mason: What Irish boy? I don't know who you're talking about.

Mother: You know who I mean. He was one of your favorites.

Mason: Impossible. You always told me not to play with the Irish kids.... *Come out of your spin.*

Mother: You know who I mean. He wrote something called *The Great Natsby.*

Mason: Gatsby! *The Great Gatsby.*

Mother: Yes. What was his name?

Mason: Albert Payson Terhune. He also wrote *Son of Gatsby, Prince: A Dog* and—

Mother: No. Fitzgibbons was his name.

Mason: You don't mean F. *Scott* Fitzgibbons?

Mother: Yes, that's the one. He was one of your favorites.

Mason: Oh, I didn't really like him that much.

Mother: Well, he made an early success.

Mason: He wrote a little trash first, and afterwards, too. ...*Now into your kicks.*

Mother: But he didn't think it was trash when he was young. I don't care what you write, if you think it's good.

Mason: *Don't give them too much ankle, dear. This is a rough crowd.*

Mother: *How's that?*

Mason: *Good. Big smile now....* *That's got 'em.* So all I have to do is lose my critical faculties. That's easy.

Mother: Nothing worth having comes easy.

Mason: A bird in the hand is worth two in the bush.

Mother: Want not, have not.

Mason: That's *waste* not, *want* not. *And you're out of step.*

Mother: Well, you're wasting and wanting too.

Mason: I won't be wanting much longer. Not at two thousand bucks a clip.

Mother: Is it making you happy?

Mason: Nothing makes me happy. I'm a malcontent.

Mother: And a perfectionist.

Mason: Yes.

Mother: And sensitive.

Mason: Of course.... *Get your knees up.*

Mother: And talented.

Mason: Why not?

Mother: A real artist.

Mason: If you like.

Mother: If *you* like.

(*Applause*)

Mason: Another ad lib. You know you're a very smartass broad, Mother.

Mother: I see your work has done fine things for your mouth.

Mason: I've been able to afford a little bridgework, if that's what you mean.

Mother: You have a fast tongue and a dirty mind, that's what I mean.

Mason: I've always had that. Now I'm getting paid to use them.... *Get the Indian clubs.*

Mother: You used to want to do better things.

Mason: I used to think the world ended at the corner of Loquat Street.

Mother: The world ends where you want it to end.

Mason: You've been dating that crazy evangelist again.

Mother: What happened to those real books you started to write?

Mason: I finished half of each of them.... *Toss them higher.*

Mother: Why didn't you finish all of one instead?

Mason: They were lousy. I couldn't tell where I left off
   and someone else began.

Mother: What did you do with them?

Mason: I burned one while listening to *La Boheme*. I got
   carried away. I still have the others. Sometimes I read
   them to my dog at night. He thinks they're lousy too.

Mother: I didn't know you had a dog. What's his name?

Mason: Bas— Bascom.

Mother: That's a good name for a dog.

Mason: Not for this one.... *Pull out the table. It's time for
   your balancing.*

Mother: Are you going to let Bascom be the judge of
   everything you write?

Mason: I'm the judge. Bascom's the bailiff.

Mother: Michael doesn't like what you're writing now
   either, does he?... *Is that thing steady?*

Mason: *Like a rock, dear.* Michael hasn't been paid to
   like it. If it were wrapped in hundred dollar bills, he'd
   like it.

Mother: And David?

Mason: The wrapping would have to be different.

Mother: And Paul and Fred? Do you think you could
   make them like it too?... *Oh, I think I'm getting dizzy.*

Mason: *You're doing fine. Just one more chair.* They'd
   like it if it were wrapped right. They've all bought it in
   one way or another.

Mother: That's why you've given up? Because you're
   disappointed in the way your friends have turned out?

Mason: A man shouldn't desert his friends.

Mother: You've got a responsibility to yourself, too.... *I
   can't do it. I'm going to fall!*

Mason: *No, you're not. Just another step.... Now let go
   with the hand...*

Mother: And... to... your... country...

Mason: *That's it! Now the flag.... Sing!*

Mother and Mason:
   O say, can you see, by the dawn's early light,

What so proudly we hailed at the twilight's last gleaming ...
And the curtain falls.

You were boffo, Mother. Write when you've got the chimps trained.
All love,

Your son,
The Prince of Wales

DECEMBER 5

December 3

Dear Mase—Just a note to ask if you got my last. Art is still waiting, drawing board in hand, to get word on that cover idea. I told him you haven't answered because you were busy finishing up the book and any day now the postman is going to surprise us with it a few days early. Well, the presses are standing by, ready to go when you are, boy. I could use a surprise like that. They knocked *Naked by Noon*, Larry's old one, off the stands in Burns, Georgia, last week. An Air Force base yet. We had K & G rush a new load right down to Macon, which is nearby, but who knows how many men can get shipped out before they get there? On top of that, nobody can find the pictures that are supposed to go in *Fifty Famous Nudes*. But Tony just finished a new book. About this woman who divorces her husband when she finds out she's a l-----n. We don't have a title yet. Any suggestions? Give them an ending that will knock their eyes out, boy. If you haven't sent the book off already.

Ben

FROM THOMAS O. LOCK

Berry, Lock & Gru
Attorneys at Law
1136 Michigan Avenue
Chicago, Illinois

Mr. Karl Vechtenmeisser
c/o Mr. Mason Greer
P.O. Box 15
Camphor, Vermont

December 3

Re: Stones

Dear Mr. Vechtenmeisser:
   We are in receipt of your second parcel which, per your instructions, is now under guard in the vault of the First National Bank of Chicago. However, in order that the proper insurance procedures and protective measures may be taken, it is necessary to have the value of your stones assessed by a mineralogist. We have taken the liberty of assigning a man to this task, and we shall inform you of the results of this assessment as soon as they are known.
   We at Berry, Lock and Gru feel most privileged that you have chosen our firm for this important service, Mr. Vechtenmeisser, and assure you that we shall do everything possible to be worthy of your confidence.
   Yours truly,

Thomas O. Lock

TOL:cj

FROM MISS NATALIE BONKERS

Monday evening

Dear Mase,

I really hadn't intended to write to you again. I'm certainly not the type of girl to keep up a correspondence with someone who doesn't want to correspond with me. But I've been thinking about that letter you wrote to Mr. Janosslit and I keep wondering if you received my reply to it. I certainly don't consider myself the world's best judge of character, but I didn't think you were the type of person to be intentionally cruel to anyone. So if you did get my letter, I can't understand why you haven't written a note of explanation, at least.

There's something else which I mention, only because it might be of some value to you. I told a boy I've been seeing lately about your letter. You may know him since he graduated from the University of Pennsylvania Law School. His name is Wallace Cooms. He told me that if I wanted to, I could actually *sue you for libel!* I don't know if you're at all familiar with libel laws, but if a damaging statement about Party A is seen by Party B, who is in a position to harm Party A, then Party A can sue Party C, the writer of the statement. Mr. Janosslit is certainly in a position to harm me in every way and Wally said I have a very good case if I wanted to sue you. Of course, I have no such intentions. But I did think you should know about the laws in such situations in case you were planning to write similar letters to other people. And I don't think that, taking all this into consideration, I am too wrong in hoping that a note of apology is too much to expect from you.

Sincerely,
Natalie

DECEMBER 6

TO MISS NATALIE BONKERS

Dec 6

Dearest woodnymph,

Why have I not written?

Can a crushed robin sing but a song of pain?

Can a bruised heart beat save in sorrowful murmurs?

I have not written because my lips are palsied by the loss of yours.

I have not written because my hands tremble with unrequited desire.

I have not written because I have waited for the changeling seasons to ease the memory of you.

But the fall leaves fell not where once you trod, and the winds did not your perfume vanish but rather were banished by it.

Now winter's first snow has come. But the barks you blessed with your touch glow whiter than all the angels' cloaks. And the snow-encrusted rock on which you sat still glows with summer warmth.

Now I know there is no escaping you. For spring will bring only rain like my tears, and summer's sun will be cold without your radiant face.

So I did not write but for my piteous Dibbs-bit of humor, a laugh torn from the breast of a clown too sad to cry.

Can you forgive that? For only the forgiveness of love can absolve the violations committed in love's name.

And you must not ask me to violate love again by writing to you, for my silence is your humble monument.

As ever and always,

M.

TO BENJAMIN WINK

Dec 6

Dear Ben:

Thanks for your notes of Nov 19, 26 and Dec 3 and Bill's book. I had intended to answer sooner, but I've been busy writing 30 pages a day. Not, unfortunately, on the book.

I'm referring to this libel thing, of course. I'm sure it won't come to anything, but the correspondence involved is epic and the mailing difficulties have kept me going up and down the mountain like a ski lift. Then there's this Martini weather, cold and dry, with regular snow flurries. I stagger back from the post office, and after an hour in front of the wood stove I feel too drowsy to do anything but sleep.

These are not excuses, of course. As you've so often said, there are no excuses for a pro except not being a pro. But with four days to deadline, I'm three weeks behind so I think you can tell Art to lower his drawing board. Furthermore, the 22 pages I've written are set at an Iowa church social so I seriously doubt if the book will contain a bedroom scene involving two Negresses. No title as yet but in accord with the embarrassment I feel, I may call it *Shame on Me.*

I guess the thing to do is use somebody else's book to fill in and I'll come in around Christmas. Sorry if this causes you any inconvenience.

About that Spragg clipping again: I am genuinely curious as to what mischief my readers are up to. If you'd send me the name of the clipping service, I'd be most grateful. Thanks, sorry and all best.

Mase

P.S. You might call Tony's book *The Gay Divorcee.*

FROM MICHAEL WESTLAKE

December 4

Dear Schoolboy:

I don't want to sound like Basil Kendricks but I think your joke with the rocks has gone far enough. Lock called today, mad as hell about it. It seems they got the idea that the rocks were worth something and had a mineralogist run a sampling on them. Needless to say, they were nothing but slag. They've tacked his fee and the delivery and storage charges onto the amount they're now asking which, incidentally, has just passed the $400,000 mark. I can only guess what you've been writing to Dibbs lately but the results speak for themselves. B. L. & G. are still in the dark about that correspondence, by the way. All they know is that every few days Dibbs calls and orders them to up the ante. They're getting a little fed up with that, too.

Let me remind you that if they decide to bow out of this thing, we stand a very good chance of facing a firm we cannot Overfelder and Thrump. As far as your plea of innocence goes, it doesn't matter whether or not you admit the truth to me. We've got to defend on the grounds of unintentional malice in any case. But we found a picture of Bibbsy in the Martha Phillips Seminary Yearbook and she is easily identifiable from your description. Then there's the references to Dibbs and his late wife which were complete idiocy on your part. I can't imagine what inspired you to chronicle them so exactly. Please spare me the answer of artistic integrity in the lower depths. I can't buy a picture of the artist peeking out from under the lavatory door. If you have some integrity, then show it by writing something decent. But writing "truths" into a trash book is as half-assed as sprinkling a decent book with trash. And this time your token integrity may cost you a bundle. If B. L. & G.

wake up in time, our whole case may rest on whether or not
Bibbsy's birthmark is a perfect trapezoid. God only knows
what land of publicity that will get. I can see the crowds
jamming the courtroom for the unveiling now.

I mentioned the possibility to Balch and it interests him.
But Wink and the higher-ups have decided to sit tight until
we have something definite. Always trying to please, I then
called the company that produced *Brandy Snifter Goes
Wild* in the hope of securing a print to see where we stood,
ass-wise. But the only prints of that classic were bought up
by the American Legion years and years ago.

In that same area, Sid has been trying to get in touch
with Bibbsy to (a) see if we can convince her to settle cheap
and (b) find out what the birthmark looks like. I'd ask you
but I know you'd say it's a tattoo of El Greco's "View of
Toledo" and art is its own justification. So far Sid's tracked
her from Aspen, Colorado to Malibu to Palm Beach and
now to Aruba. I don't know where Dibbs gets the money to
finance her travels but the phone calls are going to cost you
a tidy sum.

Finally, we got a peek at Dibbs's service record. As you
probably already know, it was distinguished by the fact that
he was kept 2,000 miles from the front at all times. Whenever
the front moved, he was moved. The reason for this can be
found in the comments made by his commanding officers
over the years. Starting with "enthusiastic," he became
progressively "adventurous," "fervent," "rabid," and,
finally, "overzealous." His overzealousness manifested itself
in a daring plan to surprise Japan with an Allied armada
creeping down from Siberia through secretly dug canals.
That got him transferred from Washington to a Navy depot
in Memphis. His retirement papers were approved the day
the war ended.

But I fail to see how we can use any of this, and if it's
news to you, I don't think you should twit Dibbs about it.

As regards the rest of your letter, I neither know nor
care about the Spragg case and I had no idea you were in
such urgent need of a Father Confessor. You may also be in

need of a lawyer if you don't start listening to instructions. Today's thoughts are: (a) tone down your letters to Dibbs (b) keep the shale out of the mail to B. L. & G. and (c) keep me posted. I'll write again as soon as I find out what else you've crapped up.

Marge, for some reason, sends love.

Mitch

DECEMBER 7

Berry, Lock & Gru
Attorneys at Law
1136 Michigan Avenue
Chicago, Illinois

Mr. Michael Westlake
c/o Targum, Rhodes, Meers 6- Meadows
Attorneys at Law
677 Fifth Avenue
New York City, N.Y.

December 5

Re: Dibbs vs. LaDouche a/k/a Greer
a/k/a Vechtenmeisser
a/k/a Bull
a/k/a Dibbs

Dear Mr. Westlake:

Due to the unexpected retirement of Mr. Lock, I have assumed the duties of chief counsel for Lt. Commander E. B. Dibbs and his daughter, Barbara Victoria. It would facilitate matters if you were to address all future correspondence to me.

Lt. Commander Dibbs has informed us that your client has continued in his private correspondence with Lt. Commander Dibbs despite our repeated requests to the contrary and despite the fact that Lt. Commander Dibbs has in no way encouraged this correspondence. Lest this suit be further complicated by a police action by Lt. Commander Dibbs against your client, I would suggest that you prohibit your client from making any further attempts to communicate with Lt. Commander Dibbs.

Yours truly,

Fenton E. Berry

FEB:cj
cc: Lt. Commander E. B. Dibbs
    Mr. Karl Vechtenmeisser

TO LT. COMMANDER E. B. DIBBS, TELEGRAM

BACKSTABBER THIS IS A DATE THAT WILL LIVE IN
INFAMY
                              VECHTENMEISSER

FROM LT. COMMANDER DIBBS, TELEGRAM

CORRESPONDENCE REVEALED BY ENEMY NURSE
PLEASE EXCUSE
                              DIBBS

TO LT. COMMANDER E. B. DD3BS

UNCONDITIONAL SURRENDER ONLY ACCEPTABLE
TERMS
                              VECHTENMEISSER

FROM LT. COMMANDER E. B. DIBBS, TELEGRAM

NUTS
                              DIBBS

DECEMBER 8

FROM BENJAMIN WINK, TELEGRAM

WHAT LIBEL THING CALL IMMEDIATELY KEEP
JABBING

BEN

FROM DAVID NOODLEMAN

Thursday

Dear Mase,

Didn't you get the last letter I wrote you? I told you to call me if you did. If you tried but couldn't reach me, try again because I've been on the run. The reason is this draft thing which is getting worse. They just upped the call to 6,000, the biggest in a year. If it's Cuba again then I am sure to get nabbed because they can put me in a uniform and get me over there in thirty minutes. I got in touch with Colonel Yapes, a very close friend of mine, but he's down with a dose he caught from his whore in Venezuela. He says there's a lot of anti-U.S. feeling down there too. If you're thinking about going in as a Conscientious Objector, you can forget it. I talked to a couple of people in the know and they said those guys have to clean up all the horseshit on the base and never get any leave. I called Monty in Hawaii, calling 200 places before I could get him, and he thinks we should all enlist together in the RAF. I don't know if he's serious or not. Anyway, he gave me a couple of numbers if we get to Havana.

Nothing else is new except Cora's sister who is staying with us is going out on her ass unless she comes up with something resembling rent. I told her maybe we could work out something and she said first I should work out by myself—a crack about a few pounds I put on. Then she told the story to Cora, only not mentioning who the guy was. You could do me a big favor if you put her in one of your books and have somebody like me rape her.

Everybody else is fine and sends their love. Call me as soon as you get this so we can figure things out. I wouldn't mind going in if we all got in the same outfit and got stationed some place like Haiti. We've got a maid from

Haiti now (# 136!) and if she is any sample, we could do much worse. Lay off the Giants Sunday. Trommlitz has a hernia.

Dave

DECEMBER 10

FROM LT. COMMANDER E. B. DIBBS,
COVER LETTER TO PARCEL

8 December

V—

Woman-in-white incident necessitates top security procedures. Enclosed find codebook to be used in future (code No. 11). Message enclosed in this code. Please answer in kind.

—D

ENCLOSURE FROM LT. COMMANDER DIBBS

FE IBXLRPHURXK PRLIOFUKRXK EW FAABUXHWL
IFX WBV UHIBEEHXP UHJRFTJH IBVXLHJ

ENCLOSURE FROM
LT. COMMANDER DIBBS, DECODED

AM CONSIDERING DISCHARGING MY ATTORNEYS
CAN YOU RECOMMEND RELIABLE COUNSEL

FROM BENJAMIN WINK

December 8

Dear Mase—Just a note to say how good it was to hear your voice today. I don't know what's wrong with Warren that he didn't tell me about this libel thing before. But like I said, you know we're going to stand behind you 100% if necessary. I blame Warren for your not getting the book in on time, and I told him so. We're running off Kenny's new one instead. About male h--------s. Kenny wanted to call it *He Wore a Yellow Ribbon*, like the song. But I say, Why ask for trouble? We're calling it A *Hungry Kind of Love*. Art is happy because he got to use his cover. Kenny wrote two Negresses into the last scene. They walk into this fella's bedroom out of the middle of nowhere and then the book is over. It doesn't make any sense to me but Kenny says it's symbolic. But the cover looks great. Wish it was on one of yours, boy. I like your church picnic idea if we can get by with it. I like *Shame on Me* too, but Art says it sounds like something kids say to each other. He came up with *Trespass Against Me* for you. What do you think? I've penciled it in now so he can start thinking about the cover. Of course it can always be changed if you come up with something better. I certainly was looking forward to reading your book this week but at least this way I'll have something to look forward to around Christmas. Thanks for your title for Tony's book. I thought it was great but Art decided it needed more zing. We're calling it *Lady Love*. Keep on top of them, boy!

Ben

P.S. About that clipping you want, we don't deal with that service any more for exactly that reason. We found out they got only one copy of each paper and sent their clients just the parts about them. Sometimes we only got one line with our name in it. It didn't make any sense, Art and I agreed. Our new service is Reliable. Do you want their address? Belt them out, boy!

Ben

DECEMBER 11

Dec 11

Dear Sir:
Enclosed please find a fragment of an article which appeared in your excellent periodical several months ago. As you can see, it concerns a party named Spragg, a collection of paperback pornography and a roomer named Bimmler. I would like to exchange this clipping for one of the complete article or for some information as to what Spragg did to make him of general newsworthiness.

I am enclosing a check for one dollar to cover any expenses you might incur in complying with this request which is of mammoth importance to me.

Thank you for your consideration and your publication's sustained contributions to journalism.

Yours truly,
Mason C. Greer

TO LT. COMMANDER E. B. DIBBS

CLG NXKDA WNZEB RJDKPONR IQBEWFSLLX
DGKKNZAIP DMOWUYB HV PCBOJRT MV
KFDAWIMXYC

TO LT. COMMANDER E. B. DIBBS, DECODED

IJK XGSPF MMXNHT UCPSZBXU RDTHYQLJJG
PKSSXNFRZ PEBYVWT OM ZITBCUA EM
SQPFYREGWI

DECEMBER 12

December 10

Dear Mase:

I assume by now you've received the carbon of Berry's letter of December 5. I believe you have every right to feel personally responsible for sending Lock out to pasture. May I now remind you that there are no other partners left in that firm? Berry is the last. The bench is bare; the dugout is deserted. If you knock him out of the box, he goes to the showers but you go to the cleaners.

I have been on the phone with Berry six times in the last three days. The situation is difficult and may be impossible. Berry is seventy-four years old and appears to be stone deaf. Our conversations run like this:

"Mr. Berry. This is Michael Westlake, counsel for Mr. Greer in Dibbs versus LaDouche a/k/a Greer a/k/a Vechtenmeisser."

"Ah, yes, Morgan. Very fine, very fine indeed. We're going to appeal your case, of course."

"I don't believe you heard me, sir. I'm calling in reference to Dibbs versus LaDouche, a defamation—"

"New information? Well, I'd be glad to hear it, of course. The cleaning woman killed us last time. No reason to believe she was still alive. No reason for her to be alive, actually."

"Mr. Berry. My name is Westlake, *West-lake.*"

"And to you, Morgan. Thanks for calling."

Of course, he might not be deaf at all. He might just be very shrewd and trying to bluff us out. I spoke to Gru who believes they have a perfect case but might be willing to settle quietly for $275,000. We know they have no case if they're going to use Overfelder and Thrump but we can't tell them that. Gru said that $275,000 is their rock bottom but I think they will take $10,000 cash. Dibbs may not like it but if we can get in touch with Bibbsy, I think she may go for it. However, Sid just lost track of her somewhere between Mobile and Tia Juana.

I can't advise you whether or not to offer $10,000. If it's you and me against Overfelder and Thrump, the case won't cost you a nickel. But if they come up with something better, it could run you $25,000. I tried to reach Balch but he's down in Washington rounding up 5,000 books which were mistakenly distributed at a political fund-raising dinner. However, Berry is certainly awake enough to raise his price if Lavatory Library is in it.

So the decision is yours. Please call or telegram your answer as soon as possible.

Mitch

TO MICHAEL WESTLAKE, TELEGRAM

OF COURSE NOT AND KEEP YOUR MOTHER AWAY
FROM MY MOTHER

GREER

DECEMBER 13

FROM LT. COMMANDER E. B. DIBBS, TELEGRAM

DO NOT HAVE ANOTHER COPY OF CODEBOOK
PLEASE COPY CODE AND RETURN BOOK

DIBBS

FROM MISS NATALIE BONKERS

Tuesday afternoon

Dearest Mase,
    I just have a minute while my children are drinking their milk to write to you. I thought your letter was one of the most beautiful things I have ever read. It reminded me of Walter de la Mare, my favorite poet. Dearest, I hope you won't mind, but I couldn't help showing your letter to Mrs. Rushing, head of the Activities Program. She thought it was wonderful and showed so much talent that she asked me if you would contribute a poem to our Arbor Day Pageant, April 22. I know it's nothing important so I thought if I wrote to you right away you'd have plenty of time to just scribble something off, preferably about trees. It certainly would do a lot to help my reputation here after that "letter," which I won't mention ever again.
    But before you even start on the poem, dearest, I want you to do a personal favor for me. Please ask Mr. Potter if my cabin is still available for this July. Surprised? I don't want to say too much about it now because July is still such a long way off and I want to save something to write about until then. I'll understand if you can't write very often but please answer this as soon as you can.
    My love to you,

                                            Natalie

FROM DR. PIETRO QUINONES

December 10

Dear Mr. Vechtenmeisser:

Lt. Commander Dibbs has informed me that you are in the process of completing my questionnaire. For this you have my gratitude and the gratitude of those who cannot speak.

In light of recent developments, I wonder if I might intrude a few additional questions.

1. Why have you begun to send cartons of rock to Lt. Commander Dibbs's attorneys?
2. How do you choose the rocks you send?
3. Is there a dominant shape among the rocks chosen?
4. What sexual significance does this shape have for you?

I have enclosed several sheets of paper for your convenience in answering these questions and I look forward to receiving them as well as the completed questionnaire shortly.

Until then, I remain,

Yours truly,
Dr. Pietro Quinones

TO LT. COMMANDER E. B. DIBBS,
COVER LETTER TO PARCEL

OHUH RL WBVU IBPHTBBS
RA RL PRQQRIVJA AB VXPHULAFXP OBY AOH
XFMW EFXFKHL AB SHHZ FQSBFA YRAOBVA WBV

TO LT. COMMANDER E. B. DIBBS, COVER
LETTER TO PARCEL, DECODED

HERE IS YOUR CODEBOOK
IT IS DIFFICULT TO UNDERSTAND HOW THE NAVY
MANAGES TO KEEP AFLOAT WITHOUT YOU

TO MISS NATALIE BONKERS

Thursday noonish

Natalie dear,

I hope you wont mind me addressing you so familiarly when we've never met, but Mase has told me so much about you that I feel we're old friends, and I surely hope we will continue to be although I'm not even sure if Mase has mentioned me to you, and the poor boy says he can't remember since we really had the most dizzy-making courtship and we were standing up at that huge altar before we really knew each other's names. My father had a stroke when he heard about it.

Anyway, among other things I'm now supposed to be Mase's private secretary if you can imagine such a thing, and, believe it or not, answering letters is something they never even talked about at Martha Phillips so I picked your letter first, simply because your handwriting is so remarkably tiny and now that Mase has told me all about you, I'm glad I did because who knows what I could say to all those publishers and people he must write to?

I'm fantastically glad that you're going to be living near us this summer because Mase told me what a marvelous cook you are and, believe it or not, after all my years *sur le Continent* I can't even boil an egg. But Mase asked me to tell you that sweet little Mr. Potter won't accept reservations for his little cabins unless you send a check, too, so I'm afraid you'll have to write to him yourself, dear, or else send us your check and Mase can give it to little Mr. Potter.

Now about your Arbor Day party which sounds absolutely fabulous, Mase said that the poem he wants to contribute is "Trees" by Joyce Kilmer. He says you should be able to find it in almost any anthology.

Well, Guess Who just yelled at me that I shouldn't spend

all day on just one letter or I'll never get caught up? But I do hope you'll write to us again soon, dear, and that we'll become very very close friends this summer.

Yours as ever,

(Mrs.) Letitia Tadcroft Greer

TO DR. QUINONES

Dec 13

Dear Dr. Quinones:

In disposing of some trash recently, I came across your questionnaire and self-administrable test which I have completed and enclosed herewith.

As regards your supplementary questions: I have been sending rocks to Lt. Commander Dibbs's attorneys because they are the cheapest and most readily obtainable heavy objects I can find. I choose the rocks for their weight but I try to remember that if a rock is too heavy, I cannot carry it. The dominant shape among the rocks chosen is oblong. The sexual significance of this shape is that I often engage in sexual intercourse on a bed which is oblong-shaped.

As you can see, I have answered this on my own paper. I have not enclosed the paper you sent me. I am keeping it.

Yours truly,
Subject V.

ENCLOSURE FROM DR. QUTNONES

I. ANSWER THE FOLLOWING QUESTIONS AS COMPLETELY AS
POSSIBLE:
A. NAME: <u>Karl Vechtenmeisser</u>
B. DATE OF BIRTH: <u>June 4, 1935</u>
C. PLACE OF BIRTH: <u>Stuttgart, Germany</u>

II. ANSWER THE FOLLOWING QUESTIONS BY CIRCLING THE
APPROPRIATE LETTER:
A. SEX: (M) F H
B. COLOR: (W) B Y R OTHER (IF OTHER, INDICATE
HERE _____)
C. MARITAL STATUS: (S) M D W

III. ANSWER THE FOLLOWING QUESTIONS BRIEFLY BUT
COMPLETELY:
A. HOW LONG HAVE YOU BEEN WRITING PORNOGRAPHY?
<u>Professionally, about two years; on a</u>
<u>amateur basis, off and on since I was seven.</u>
B. DESCRIBE THE FIRST PIECE OF PORNOGRAPHY YOU
WROTE: <u>Dirty poem.</u>
_____
C. WHY DO YOU FEEL YOU WROTE IT? _____
<u>Self-expression.</u>
D. WRITE AS MUCH OF IT AS YOU CAN REMEMBER. (USE
SEPARATE SHEET IF NECESSARY, OR ENCLOSE COPY OF
PIECE IF POSSIBLE) <u>Roses are Red;Violets are</u>
<u>Blue; Francine Hargester; Screws. Do you?</u>
E. WHAT WAS YOUR AGE WHEN YOU WROTE THIS PIECE
OF PORNOGRAPHY? <u>Seven years.</u>
_____
F. DID YOU SHOW IT TO ANYONE? IF SO, HOW? _____
<u>Wrote it on lavatory wall.</u>

G. WHAT WAS YOUR OPINION OF THIS PIECE OF PORNOGRAPHY AT THE TIME YOU WROTE IT? _____
Very good.

H. WHAT IS YOUR OPINION OF THIS PIECE OF PORNOGRAPHY NOW ? _____
Childish.

I. WHAT CHANGES WOULD YOU MAKE IN IT NOW?_____
None.

J. HOW LONG WAS IT AFTER YOU COMPLETED THIS PIECE OF PORNOGRAPHY UNTIL YOU ENGAGED IN SEXUAL INTERCOURSE? Eleven years.

K. WHAT TYPE OF SEXUAL INTERCOURSE DID YOU ENGAGE IN? Screwing.

L. IN WHAT WAY WAS THE PORNOGRAPHIC WORK RELATED TO THAT ACT OF SEXUAL INTERCOURSE? _____
Partner was mentioned in composition.

IV. FILL IN THE BLANKS IN THE FOLLOWING SENTENCES WITH THE FIRST WORD OR WORDS THAT COME TO MIND.
A. MY FAVORITE PART OF THE BODY IS THE ___head___
B. THREE THINGS I LIKE TO DO WITH THIS PART ARE ___think___ AND ___see___ AND _hold up hats_
C. MY PRIVATE NAME FOR THIS PART IS ___"Heady"___

V. ANSWER THE FOLLOWING QUESTIONS BRIEFLY BUT COMPLETELY:
A. DESCRIBE THE MOST RECENT PIECE OF PORNOGRAPHY YOU WROTE: Dirty book.

B. WHY DO YOU FEEL YOU WROTE IT? _____
Self-expression and money.

C. WRITE AS MUCH OF IT AS YOU CAN REMEMBER. (USE SEPARATE SHEET IF NECESSARY OR ENCLOSE COPY OF PIECE IF POSSIBLE) Book enclosed.

D. WHAT WAS YOUR AGE WHEN YOU WROTE THIS PIECE
OF PORNOGRAPHY? <u>Twenty-seven years.</u>
_____

E. DID YOU SHOW IT TO ANYONE? IF SO, HOW? _____
<u>Published by Scepter Books; distributed</u>
<u>by K & G Magazine Agency.</u>

F. WHAT WAS YOUR OPINION OF THIS PIECE OF
PORNOGRAPHY AT THE TIME YOU WROTE IT? _____
<u>Very good.</u>

G. WHAT IS YOUR OPINION OF THIS PIECE OF
PORNOGRAPHY NOW? _____
<u>Childish.</u>

H. WHAT CHANGES WOULD YOU MAKE IN IT NOW? _____
<u>Delete name "Dibbs."</u>

I. HOW LONG WAS IT AFTER YOU COMPLETED THIS PIECE
OF PORNOGRAPHY UNTIL YOU ENGAGED IN SEXUAL
INTERCOURSE? _____
<u>Time still elapsing.</u>

J. WHAT TYPE OF SEXUAL INTERCOURSE DID YOU
ENGAGE IN? _____
_____

K. IN WHAT WAY WAS THE PORNOGRAPHY WORK RELATED
TO THAT ACT OF SEXUAL INTERCOURSE? _____
<u>May have prevented it.</u>

VI. BY DRAWING LINES, CONNECT THE WORDS IN THE
FOLLOWING COLUMNS IN THE WAY WHICH SEEMS MOST
LOGICAL TO YOU:

MOTHER	FORK
BED	SISTER
FATHER	BLACK
BODY	BROTHER
WHITE	HEAD
KNIFE	PILLOW

VII. BELOW ARE THE FIRST SENTENCES OF THREE DIFFERENT
STORIES. ON A SEPARATE SHEET OF PAPER, WRITE EACH
OF THESE SENTENCES AND THEN COMPLETE THE STORIES
IN ANY MANNER YOU WISH.

A. A YOUNG MAN WALKED INTO A PHARMACY. HE WAITED
UNTIL ALL THE OTHER CUSTOMERS HAD LEFT. THEN
HE APPROACHED THE WOMAN BEHIND THE COUNTER.

B. A MAN AND A WOMAN ARE IN BED TOGETHER. THEY
ARE BOTH DISTURBED ABOUT SOMETHING.

C. TWO BOYS ARE PLAYING IN A DARK CELLAR.

A. A young man walked into a pharmacy. He waited until all the other customers had left. Then he approached the woman behind the counter.

"I'd like a sirloin steak, potatoes and coffee, please," he said. "Make the steak rare."

"We don't have no steaks," said the woman. "This is a pharmacy, not a restaurant."

"I'd like a cabin cruiser then," said the young man. "Twin bunks."

"We don't have any boats. I told you, this is a pharmacy."

"So that's the way it is," said the young man. "Whatever I want, you don't have." He reached into his coat and produced a pistol.

The woman screamed. A boy came running in from the back. "What's up?" he asked.

"Your hands, if you're smart," said the young man. "What time does the Swede come in?"

"What Swede?"

"Any Swede."

"Six-forty."

"Smart boy," said the young man.

B. A man and a woman are in bed together. They are both disturbed about something.

"Darling," the woman says, "I have something terrible to tell you."

"What?"

"Well, you know how badly we've needed money and you've been working so late and—well, first look under your pillow."

"A present! For me?"

"Yes."

"But how did you get the money?"

"Well—"

"Oh, never mind. Now you look under your pillow."

"Oh, darling! You shouldn't have. But where did you ever get the money?"

"It's not important."

"Oh, Merry Christmas, darling."

"Merry Christmas, yourself."

C. Two boys are playing in a dark cellar. The
older boy clamps the younger one in chains and
walls him up.

DECEMBER 14

FROM DAVID NOODLEMAN, TELEGRAM

WHAT GIVES WHY HAVEN'T YOU CALLED CALL

DAVE

TO DAVID NOODLEMAN

Dec 14

Dear Cora's Sister's Brother-in-Law:
    I have not called because I could not bear to hear your suntanned voice and the palm trees rustling like crisp currency and the harpstring ripples of the blue Atlantic. It is 10 above zero here. A nymphomaniac wind beats on my door and her wanton sisters claw at my windows. Snow has been falling dropsically for six days and tomorrow is red-circled on my calendar as Blizzardkrieg. There is no doubt in all of Camphor, or in me, that heavy snow will be on us ere long. I have compiled a lengthy list of needed supplies, and upon completing this letter, I shall hie down to the store and purchase them. That is why I have not called.
    Besides, I have nothing to say to you. Your draft delusions are just that, probably brought on by change of life. Consult your gynecologist. However, I can see where the country is in big trouble if Hockstader uses the same toilet as a colonel with Venezuelan clap. We may well be within one flush of a nuclear war.
    It may interest you to know that I have renewed my correspondence with one Michael Westlake, attorney for the Ku Klux Klan. He claims to have met you at a recent barbeque. At least he described you to my satisfaction: a stocky coconut-complexioned man addicted to scratching his bottom. If you have altered your appearance, send me a new photo for my dresser. We are in communion for business purposes, the Good Lawyer Westlake and I. He is determined to purge me of my sins against Literature by divesting me of some $10,000 in a libel action. Then, he says, I shall be pure enough to pursue my true calling, writing confession stories for *Catholic Digest*. However, I resist him.

From the Green Mountains to the Seagram Building, the earth trembles from our titanic struggle.

Meanwhile, somewhere in the South Pacific, a lunatic Naval Commander peers wildly through his periscope searching for latent Nazis.

"One hundred thousand," he barks.

"Two hundred thousand," corrects his daughter.

"Three hundred thousand," shrieks the Commander.

"Four hundred thousand," insists his nurse.

"There she blows!" remarks the Commander of his daughter.

The crew smirks.

"Fire Gru," shouts the Commander.

"Gru fired, sir."

"Fire Lock!"

"Lock fired, sir."

"Hire Berry!"

"Berry hired, sir."

Whooosh, Gru snakes through the water. Kaploommm! He explodes against Oren Overfelder. Swooosh, Lock spirals through the depths. Garrunnch! He runs aground on two cartons of rock. Zwooooosh, Berry is headed right for me. And I have orders not to defend myself. Now you're up to date.

Your tip on Trommlitz' crotch came just in time. I had $30,000 riding on that area. Forthwith, I dispatched a cable to my bookmaker, Blinky Wink, and transferred my wager to the Colts. Unfortunately, Rzeppa seems to use the same toilet as Trommlitz.

Congratulations on #136. Keep jabbing, fella!

Mase

DECEMBER 16

TO MICHAEL WESTLAKE

Dec 16

Dear Counselor:

You've been doing such a crackerjack job on my defense
that I hesitate to mention I was arrested by the F.B.I. today.
This is the truth. Enclosed is a copy of the statement I signed.
The formal police report of the ceremonies will be sent to
you if Sergeant Polk of the Haute Verde Police Department
inserts the carbon paper right side up; if not, your copy will
be on the back of the Haute Verde P.D. copy. In either case,
Sergeant Polk's manuscript is likely to lack the color and
verve that an eyewitness could bring to the narrative. So,
while everything is fresh as footprints...

It snowstormed here yesterday, exactly as predicted by
this columnist six weeks ago. It was an efficient, methodical
snowstorm; it covered the ground, the trees, the housetops,
the roads, and then it stopped. When I awoke this morning
the snow was banked to my windows. A leftover wind sent
feathery fingers to goose me through the cracks in the walls.
I wanted nothing more than to read my Sunday *Times* but
only if A. H. Sulzberger himself brought it to my door. I was
not going outside for anything. Creeping around the cabin
wearing my electric blanket, I made coffee, turned on the
radio, arranged the dog over my feet and sat listening to the
Reverend Barkeley Uzzell of the First Church of Christian
Fellows explain why Jesus could not wait forever for me.
(He gives priority to new sinners.) Outside the wind showed
off by bending some pine trees and dared me to come out
and Indian-wrestle. I spelled out my reply on the steamed
panes and the wind and Reverend Uzzell roared.

At about ten there was a knock on my door. There had been, I learned later, knocks during the several previous minutes. I opened the door and was considerably more surprised to find that my visitor was wearing a cotton cord suit than that he was from the F.B.I. His name was Agent #178732 (ne Arnold Eisentraub); he had come all the way from Los Angeles and he was almost frozen stiff. I invited him in and he accepted without formality. In view of his occupation, I will describe him only as being of my age, average height and nondescript. I gave him some coffee, my electric blanket and my place in front of the stove. He used all three for several silent, shivering minutes. When he felt well enough to speak, his first question was, "Do you know a Mason Clark Greer?"

I told him I hadn't spoken to Greer for some time but I assumed we were still on friendly terms.

"Will you just answer the question?" he said, rather peevishly. "I don't like this any more than you do, you know."

I told him that I knew Greer. He then explained that Greer had been reported missing and a high-ranking Army official had initiated an F.B.I. search for him. That, he said, was as much as he could tell, the remainder of his knowledge being part of a confidential report he had been handed seven hours before at the Los Angeles Airport and of which he did not understand a word. He then asked me if I knew a Karl Vechtenmeisser, a ski instructor reported to be living in the neighborhood.

That brought things into some sort of focus so I confided as much of our little story as I thought could be believed.

Agent Eisentraub listened with no great interest, drinking two more cups of coffee and smoking half a pack of cigarettes. When I had finished, he said, "Well, that sounds just like the futting Bureau. I haven't been on one case yet that's panned out. I think I'm going to arrest you anyway."

I told him I understood how those things were.

"It's only a temporary arrest," he explained, crumpling his empty pack of cigarettes and borrowing a butt from me. "Just to get you down to the nearest authorities for an official statement and the answers to the questions on that report. If I still *have* that futting report. Some woman sitting next to me on the plane got off at Denver and took my manual, my magazines and who the hell knows what else."

I told him of a similar experience I had undergone on a train to Boston and asked him what "futting" meant.

"What it sounds like," he said. "It's Bureau slang. Hoover's orders. Lets the boys sound like men without offending anybody. By the way, where are the nearest authorities?"

"There's a police station in Haute Verde."

"I guess now I'm supposed to guess where Haute Verde is, huh?"

"It's about thirty miles from here."

"Great. You can drive us there in my car while I get some sleep."

"How do I get back?"

"I'll run you back if we don't keep you overnight. I'd say take two cars but I'm not supposed to let you out of my sight. Besides, I'm too tired to drive and why should you waste your gas? Let the futting Bureau pay for it."

That sounded fair and I asked if I could bring Bastard.

"Why not? He's not a Doberman, is he?"

"No. Weimaraner."

"Then okay. I hate Dobermans. They use them in training school and one of them almost tore my leg off."

I assured him Bastard was untrained; he had a few more of my cigarettes while I dressed and we bundled off.

In the event you haven't experienced it, the drive from my cabin to anywhere is downhill over an unpaved corkscrew road. Overhanging ledges had caught most of the snow intended for the road but in some places there were thick dunes which, until Agent Eisentraub crashed through them earlier, were impassable. His car was a Chevrolet he had rented at the Burlington Airport and the shocks were bad. In addition, I was unused to driving an automatic shift and displayed a tendency to throw us into second (reverse on an automatic shift) every so often. Agent Eisentraub soon abandoned his plan to sleep and renewed his discussion of the F.B.I.

"They've got about as much organization as the Yeshiva High football team" (on which he played right guard), he explained. "You know how they pick agents for an assignment? On a seniority basis. The older, experienced men sit around all day playing pinochle and the new boys like me catch all the crap. Like *this*. All the way from L.A. last night. Now that they got jets, they don't care where they pull the men from. What's a couple of hours more or less? Nobody's ever expecting you anyway. I'll bet my boss hasn't been out of L.A. in the last ten years, except for vacations. You know where I've been just in the last two months?" He ticked them off on his fingers. "Eustis, Colorado; Communist conspiracy suspected: negative; Batley Falls, Alabama; narcotics ring suspected: negative; Grocer's Bluff, Kansas; national bookmaking syndicate suspected: negative. And now, you. I don't even know what you're supposed to have done."

"Illegal possession of Selective Service Card," I said. "Negative."

The Camphor postmaster was shoveling the walk before his liquor store when we stopped at a light.

"Hi," he nodded.

"Hi," I nodded back.

"Going for a ride?" he asked.

"Arrested," I said.

He nodded wisely, the light changed and we drove on.

From Camphor to Haute Verde, the early traffic had cleared the highway. The road was level and four-laned. Although Haute Verde is a quiet, frostbitten town of only 3,000, it is the hub of the state's highway system and directly linked with all of New England's through-ways. The former governor of Vermont was born in Haute Verde.

We arrived about noon. The police station was closed, but Agent Eisentraub used his position to get Chief of Police Crapaud to come over and open it for us. Chief Crapaud, who greatly resembles Dave Noodleman's Uncle Murray and the late Mayor La Guardia, was not pleasantly disposed to do this. The imposition aside, Chief Crapaud did not rank the F.B.I. very high in his esteem. In 1956, he had written a personal letter to Director Hoover asking if Hoover might not pull a few strings to enable the Chief's daughter to sing "The Star Spangled Banner" at the opening game of the World Series. He had not yet received a reply.

He informed us of this as he stamped the snow off his boots and parka and led us into his austere, cellular office. There we found two gun-metal desks, three gun-metal chairs and several gun-metal cabinets. Chief Crapaud turned on the heater, seated himself behind one of the desks and directed his interest to the Catholic Church across the street. Agent Eisentraub requested some paper and a stenographer to write on it.

"Paper's in one of the cabinets," said the chief without turning from the window. "No stenographer. No tape recorder, phone taps or one-way mirrors either. You or your prisoner can type up the thing, with one carbon for us, and I'll have my sergeant make up a report from it and send you a copy. Maybe. I won't promise, because Polk has trouble deciding which side of the carbon paper goes up."

"We won't need a copy," said Eisentraub quietly.

"His lawyer might," said the chief. "You given him a chance to call one yet?"

"Would you like to call your lawyer?" Eisentraub asked me.

"I don't think so," I said. "I'd rather not bother him."

"Would you mind doing the typing? I can hardly keep my eyes open."

Chief Crapaud snorted.

"I don't mind," I said. "I'll give you the answers as I type them."

Which is just what I did, making one copy for the chief and one for you. As you can see, all the questions concerned my relationship with Karl Vechtenmeisser so I amended them slightly so that my answers might seem coherent. Eisentraub looked it over and said it was fine. I signed as

Suspect; Eisentraub signed as Agent and Chief Crapaud signed as Witness. Then Eisentraub had a standard set of loyalty questions he was obliged to ask. The first one was: Do you know of any persons who are members of the Communist Party?

"Well, there's Nikita Khrushchev, of course," I said.

"If you only knew how many times I've heard that," Eisentraub said wearily.

"Shouldn't ask it in such a stupid way then," said Chief Crapaud.

"My orders," said Eisentraub stiffly, "are to read the questions the way they're written."

"They order you to wear a cotton suit in the middle of winter, too?" inquired the chief.

"They don't supply us with cowboy hats," said Eisentraub pointedly.

"Probably can't get them in size six," retorted the chief.

"Hick cop," said Eisentraub under his breath and asked the rest of the loyalty questions which I answered directly to avoid further arguments.

"The whole thing's a waste of time," opined Chief Crapaud. "F.B.I. never won a case that I know of."

"I'll go along with that," said Eisentraub.

"Oh," said Chief Crapaud, swiveling from the window, "so you're not a company man after all."

"Just earning my salary," said Eisentraub. "Same as you."

"Same as me, eh?" said the chief. "Well then, how do you feel about drinking on duty?"

"Is that an invitation?" asked Eisentraub, tough as Bogart.

"Is that an affirmative response?" countered Crapaud, sly as Greenstreet.

"Put out a bottle and you'll see," said Eisentraub.

The chief produced a very full fifth of Jack Daniel's from his drawer, unplugged it and set it down on the desk with a thud. Eisentraub chug-a-lugged three gulps without taking his eyes off Crapaud and set the bottle down. Crapaud took it and tossed back four swallows without taking his eyes off

Eisentraub. When he set the bottle down, they both broke into silly laughter.

"What about your prisoner?" said the chief. "He human, too?"

"He's not my prisoner any more," said Eisentraub. "I'm all finished with him."

"You human?" inquired the chief.

"Is that an invitation?" I asked.

The Chief waved grandly at the bottle. I poured down four mouthfuls, not taking my eyes off anybody. Then all three of us laughed together.

"Pull up a chair," said the chief. "You can help me watch the Catholics."

We did just that, passing around the bottle as we watched.

"Catholics fascinate me," said the chief. "I could watch them all day. Either of you Catholics by any chance?"

Eisentraub revealed that he was Jewish but hadn't practiced much since he joined the F.B.I. I admitted that I was between Gods at the moment.

"You can't belong to the Bureau unless you profess some religious belief," said Eisentraub. "There's no pressure on you to become a Jew, of course."

"I was born a Methodist, married an Episcopalian and got a daughter who's married to a Baptist," said the chief. "You ask me, they're all the same."

"I was going to be a rabbi once," said Eisentraub. "I even went to Yeshiva High School. Then I took an aptitude test that showed I was low in Religion and Social Work and high in Sports and Law Enforcement. So my mother made me join the F.B.I."

"I guess the F.B.I.'s not really so bad, except for those stupid suits they make you wear."

"I just came from Los Angeles," Eisentraub explained.

"My wife and I went to Cleveland last summer," said the chief. "That's even less of a town than Haute Verde. What's your trade?" he asked me. "You *look* like a *kidnapper*."

"No," I said. "I write pornography."

"Now really. Any hot ones?"

"A few."

"We don't get too much of that around here. Polk goes all the way to Burlington for his. You write under any particular name?"

"Guy LaDouche."

"Yeah, I believe Polk's got some of your stuff. He had quite a collection at one time but then he got married and his wife gave them all away to the Goodwill."

"Well, at least they won't go to waste," I said. "Somebody will get to read them."

"Had a pornography case not long ago," said Eisentraub. "Segovia, North Dakota: negative."

"Never met a pornographer before," said the chief. "I always thought you fellows were generally older."

"I'm one of the youngest."

"Well, it's a living, I guess. Somebody's got to do it. I'd guess it gets pretty tiresome after a while, though."

"Yes, it does."

"Figured it would. Unless all those things really happened to you. Do they?"

"No. I make them up."

"That's what I told Polk. But he said you couldn't write about them like that unless they really happened to you. Polk's quite a fan of yours. You might like to meet him sometime. Except he's very stupid."

"Bottle's almost empty," said Eisentraub.

Chief Crapaud attended to that by calling Polk and ordering him to report to the station immediately with two fifths of Jack Daniel's and nine sandwiches in custody. "Make it twelve sandwiches if you haven't eaten," he added, and hung up.

"Now you'll get to meet Polk," he said to me. "He's all right, except he's very stupid. A Baptist, like my son-in-law.... Well, there go the last of them. We missed the first mass. My house is two streets over so I can see them right from my window. If I'm up on Sunday, I like to watch both masses.... Behind those books on top of that cabinet, I believe you'll find some cider we can use while we're waiting for Polk."

I found it and we used it. Eisentraub took one sip and then fell asleep with the jug in his lap.

"We had a Catholic woman in here last spring," said the chief. "Homicide. Shot her husband. I tried to talk to her about the Catholics but she just sat in the cell and cried all the time. Very odd group."

"Minorities tend to be clannish," I said.

"Yeah. I've noticed that," said the chief. "We've got three Negro boys here in town, thick as thieves."

Presently Polk arrived with the supplies. He was a tall, thin young man who seemed very pleased to be of service. "Chief," he said with a snappy salute.

"Open a bottle," said his superior.

"Yes, sir," said Polk. "I think you'll be pleased with me, Chief. I just gave out a parking ticket."

"Not my car again, I hope," said the chief.

"No, sir. This was a blue Chevrolet, illegally parked right in front of the station."

"Was there a weimaraner in it?" I asked.

"If that's a dog, yes sir, there might have been. There was some sort of dog in there. I couldn't tell you what kind."

"That's Eisentraub's car," I said to the chief.

"Tear up the ticket, Polk. Car belongs to the man sleeping over there. He's from the F.B.I."

"About your daughter, sir?"

"No," said the chief. "You ever gonna get that bottle open?"

"Yessir. You want the sandwiches now too, sir?"

"Yes," said the chief. "I think they might go very well with lunch."

Polk handed round the sandwiches, putting Eisentraub's in his lap.

"This gentleman is Mr. Guy LaDouche," the chief told Polk. "Mr. LaDouche, Sergeant Polk."

"How do you do," said Polk. We shook hands.

"Mr. LaDouche's name doesn't mean anything to you?" the chief asked Polk.

"No, sir. Unless he's that bank robber. Is he, sir?"

"No," said the chief. "Mr. LaDouche is the famous pornographer."

"Oh," said Polk. "Well, I'm afraid I don't know very much about the sport."

"Mr. LaDouche writes the dirty books you read, Polk."

"Oh, now, Chief. I don't think it's right to tell people about those."

"Mr. LaDouche knows somebody reads them, Polk. Otherwise he wouldn't be writing them. Isn't that right, Mr. LaDouche?"

"Absolutely. How do you like the books, Polk?"

"Very well, sir."

"Do you remember reading any of mine?"

"Well, to tell you the truth, sir, one book is pretty much the same as the next to me."

"Then why do you drive to Burlington every week to buy new ones?" asked the chief.

"Well, once I know how the book comes out, I've got no interest in reading it again, sir."

"The endings are the most important thing to you," I said.

"No, sir. I like the dirty parts. But once I know how and where and things like that, well, it's just like doing it yourself, if you know what I mean. I sort of lose interest."

"I think you put that very well," I said.

"I don't," said the chief. He picked a sliver of Swiss cheese from his teeth. "Don't you have anything you'd like to ask Mr. LaDouche, Polk?"

"No, sir. Do you want me to leave now? I haven't finished my sandwiches yet."

"You'll have to excuse Polk," the chief said to me. "He's very stupid.... Polk, whenever we talk about these books, you always say to me, 'Boy, if the guy who wrote this were here, I'd like to ask him one question. Just one.' That's what you always say, Polk. Now do you remember that question?"

"Yes sir. Do you want me to ask Mr. LaDouche?"

"Do you want to know the answer, Polk?"

"No, sir."

"Then why do you always say, 'Boy, if the guy who wrote this—'"

"Excuse me, sir," said Polk. "But I say that because I know Mr. LaDouche isn't there. I don't really want to know if the things he writes about really happened to him. If that's the question you mean, sir."

"That's the one, Polk. That's the one. If you've asked it once, you've asked it a thousand times. *Now why in hell don't you want to know the answer?*"

"Because I'm afraid he'll say no, sir. And then I wouldn't like the books any more."

"Why would that make such a difference to you?" I asked Polk. "The books would be the same whether you knew the things had really happened or not, wouldn't they? They'd still have the illusion of reality, if they were any good."

"Yes, sir, I suppose they would. And your books are good, sir. I think they're probably the best ones I've read."

"Thank you."

"But if I knew that those things didn't really happen, sir, then I'd think the books would be sort of dishonest, if you know what I mean. Sort of lying in a way, sir. I know that most books are made up but you *know* that. I mean you know when you're reading the book that the writer doesn't want you to believe it completely. I mean, you know that he's just telling a story and he doesn't expect you to get all hotted up about it. I mean you *can* get all hotted up if you want but it's not necessary, if you know what I mean."

"I think I do," I said. "But why are the kind of books that I write different?"

"Because idiots like Polk read them," said the chief. "Have a drink."

"No, thank you, sir," said Polk. "Not while I'm on duty."

"I wasn't talking to you," said the chief. "Here you go, LaDouche." He handed the bottle to me and watched admiringly as I swigged it.

"Nobody drinks like a Frenchman. Right, LaDouche?"

"Right."

"What part of France are you from?"

"I'm from Philadelphia."

"Never heard of it. I'm from near Quebec myself."

"There's a Philadelphia in Pennsylvania," said Polk.

"That's the one I'm from," I said.

"I thought you said you were French," said the chief, taking the bottle back. "LaDouche is a goddamned French name."

"That's not my real name," I said. "My name is Greer."

"Guy Greer," said the chief speculatively. "Well, that sounds French enough." He handed the bottle back. "Here, Greer. Hey! A rhyme. Here, Greer, more beer." He smiled delightedly. "Not bad. Here, Greer, never fear, more beer..."

"Excuse me, sir," said Polk, "but that's whiskey. I thought you said you wanted—"

"Oh shut up, Polk!"

"Yes, sir."

"Why are the kind of books that I write different from the others that don't have to be real to you?" I asked Polk.

"Well, sir... Can I answer him, Chief?"

"You can do whatever you like, Polk. I just fired you."

"Oh, why, sir?"

"Because nothing rhymes with your name."

"Yolk," I said.

"And folk," said Polk. "Back home, they called my family the Polk folk."

"Bulk," said the chief. "And culk. You're hired again, Polk."

"I think that's pronounced caulk," I said.

"And sulk," said the chief happily. "Polk, I'm going to make you a captain."

"Thank you, sir. Can I answer Mr. Greer's question now?"

"Only if you want to, Polk. You're a police officer, remember that. He's just a civilian pornographer. Make him show you some respect."

"Yes, sir... I want to answer your question now, Mr. Greer."

"I'd appreciate it if you would, Mr. Polk."

"*Captain* Polk, you dirty writer," said the chief.

"Captain Polk," I said.

"It's because your books are about sex, sir. Mostly about sex, anyway. And I take my sex very seriously, sir, if you know what I mean."

"Polk," said the chief, "you're a *billygoat*! Do you know that?"

"Yes sir. I guess I do. I mean my wife has said pretty much the same thing to me."

"How is your wife?" asked the chief.

"Very well, thank you, sir."

"I bet I know what you two were doing when I called you.

"I was sleeping, sir. And my wife was knitting."

"Then why is your fly open, Polk?"

"Excuse me, sir, but I believe that's Mr. Greer's fly you're looking at."

"You know, Polk, I think you're right. Are you married, Greer?"

"I think I'd better be going," I said, standing and zipping up.

"Polk, if the prisoner tries to escape, shoot him."

"Is Mr. Greer our prisoner, sir?"

"No," I said.

"Yes!" said the chief. "All Catholics are my prisoners. I'm going to lock them up and study them."

"I'm not Catholic," I said.

"Then get the hell out of here! And take that F.B.I. stooge with you... There's nothing wrong with my daughter's voice. Hoover's just jealous."

I roused Eisentraub and tried to get him to his feet.

"Do you want me to help you, sir?" asked Polk.

"You'll help nobody," said the chief. "You're a servant of the people. Remember that. Now go out and arrest some Catholics."

"Yes, sir. About how many?"

"Depends how big they are. How do Catholics usually run?"

"I've known some who were very big, sir. And then I've seen some babies who were quite small."

"Well, get me a couple of each."

"Yes, sir. About how many?"

They were still discussing it as I hauled Eisentraub, his briefcase and your copy of the statement out to the car.

It is now eight-thirty in the evening. Eisentraub and Bastard are curled like quotation marks on my bed. I may or may not wash the dinner dishes before I join them. Probably negative.

I am enclosing also the latest set of communications with Dibbs. As you can see, we are on the closest of terms. I spoke to Wink a week ago Saturday. Until then he knew nothing of the suit. You might consider Warren Balch as a prospective partner for your firm. You are doing, I repeat, an absolutely crackerjack job for me.

Your client,

Attila

DECEMBER 17

December 14

Dear Mase:

While plotting our courtroom strategy against B. L. & G., I came across a small technicality which I thought might be worth passing along.

The complaint against you is illegal.

Its an error that only a seventeen-year-old law clerk would make and three guesses who pointed it out to me. (His name is Brewster Teal and he will, undoubtedly, be head of the Supreme Court before he is twenty.) It's the first thing you learn in law school: service of a complaint must be delivered to the defendant in person unless he resides in the same state as the plaintiff. With you in Vermont and Dibbs in Illinois, the mail is not considered an authorized carrier. A Vermont agent such as a J. P. or a police officer would have to bring you the bad news in person. The only other alternative would be for you to go to Illinois to get served. I would not advise you to consider such trips until this thing is over.

So, now we just sit tight, let B. L. & G. take us to a hearing, then coldcock them. To that purpose, please don't do anything that might discourage an early showdown. If it's at all possible, be humble and compliant. Agree to anything Dibbs asks—except a visit to him. You may just get out of this free yet.

Daniel Webster

FROM BENJAMIN WINK

December 15

Dear Mase—Just a note to make sure you got my last with that title for you, *Trespass Against Me.* Art liked it so much he stayed up all weekend knocking out the cover and it looks great, fella. This naked blonde girl is leaning over this altar where this priest in a hood is about to stick two knives into her breasts. There are a bunch of religious signs and marks all around and if you can work them in, too, all the better. I've got a feeling this one will be your greatest yet, boy. Bill brought in a new one, *We Five Lovers,* but we set it up without even reading it. Bill's books are always the same, not that that is bad, but they're nothing special like yours. Well, I haven't heard from Warren for a while about that libel thing so I guess its over and just as well the way I see it. I don't think an artist can do his best work with something like that hanging over him. Take my advice, boy, and leave it to the lawyers next time. Finish them off, fella!

Ben

DECEMBER 18

TO MICHAEL WESTLAKE

Dec 18

Dear Mitch:

It's encouraging to know you're right up there with the seventeen-year-old law clerks. Hypothetically, what would have happened if I had agreed to settle out of court for ten grand? Hypothetically, I think I would have been out ten grand. You can deduct your fee from that and give the rest to Brewster Teal for his judge's habit.

Nothing from Dibbs in a while and I hope my luck holds. My daily problems are enough. It is ball-freezing cold here now, Bastard whines incessantly and, as a special added attraction, F.B.I. Agent Eisentraub is back with us. The background of that is not without interest:

On Monday morning, blessed with a staggering hangover, Agent E. bade me farewell and departed into the snowy bleakness. About noon, while collecting firewood and trying to lose Bastard, I noticed some footprints other than our own. They were shod and appeared to be human but they formed no intelligent pattern, charging off in one direction only to wander back from another, inscribing pointless circles, hooks and stunted arabesques. Like students of some deranged dance teacher, Bastard and I followed the trail up to the wooded hillock overlooking my cabin. There the tracks darted about a bit before leading to a ring of pines on a dead-end ledge. And there, asleep in the deep of his prints, we found Agent E.

Bastard awakened him with a near-miss urination and he sprang up at me with excessive heartiness—"Hey, hey! How are you?"—grasping my mittened hand as though we were

on the convention floor. When I expressed wonderment
that he was back, he swatted snow from the pants of his
suspiciously new snowsuit and said, "Well, you know how
it goes. Gone today, here tomorrow."

"What for?" I asked.

"Oh, Bureau business," he said with jaunty vagueness,
and bent to pat Bastard whom I knew he detested.

"I take it it's about my case," I said.

"Why do you say that?"

"Oh, call it egotism, but I happen to be the only human
being for ten miles."

He chuckled strenuously but offered no further
enlightenment. After a while we parted; I still bemused, he
with a wave that was toujours gai.

That was about noon. At two, while sweeping some snow
from the roof, I noticed him camped behind a thicket of
scruffy trees, eating what appeared to be canned rations
from a kit similar to those issued to downed fliers. He did
not see me. Then at five, while on a constitutional, I ran into
him again, skulking some twenty yards behind me.

"Hi there!" he cried upon being noticed and jogged up to
me, the only other guest at the resort. "Taking a little walk?"
he asked.

"No," I said. "I'm on a secret mission for the Czar."

He slapped my back appreciatively and asked if I minded
his company. I told him I didn't mind it but I wouldn't object
to having it explained either. For a moment he looked as if
he were on the verge of another buffoon's sally, but then the
air went out of him and he turned contrite. "Oh, what's the
use? I don't know how the fut the Bureau expects anyone to
handle a case like this."

"Like what?"

"You. I'm supposed to be following you."

"Well, you're doing a helluva job. I don't think we've been
out of each other's sight for a minute all day." But he looked
so fretful that I was sorry I had said it. "Is my case coining
along badly?" I asked.

"Under surveillance," he mumbled, kicking at a mound of snow.

"What does that mean?"

"It means they don't know what the fut they're doing. Whenever they don't know what else to do, they put a case under surveillance. Spies, bankrobbers, junkies. We got a man covering every one of them. You want to know where your tax dollar is going, you're paying some poor bastard to follow a junkie all day."

"Today it seems that I'm paying to have myself tailed," I said.

"And I would be the one to draw it. I always catch the shit. Without ten or twelve years, you're nothing in the Bureau."

"How many years do you have?"

"Six. I joined right out of the service. That's the best way to do it. You get out in civilian life and get used to keeping your own hours and not taking orders and all that Mickey Mouse horseshit and you never want to go back. Most of the boys joined right out of the service. Then we've got a couple who played pro ball for a while. You remember Zazz Stdelski, used to be linebacker for the Steelers?"

"No."

"Well, he's with us. Number 178703. Joined up just before me."

I asked him what his number was again.

"178732. But that has nothing to do with when you joined. It just happened to turn out that way with me and Zazz. Your number designates a few things which are classified information. When a man retires his number can be put back in circulation and given to somebody else. With the exception of some of the great Bureau boys like George T. Dompler or William R. Alloky. In those cases, they retire the number with the man, like baseball players."

"I don't think I ever heard of Dompler or Alloky."

"The best Bureau boys are the ones you don't hear about," he said firmly. "Dompler helped catch 'Baby Face' Nelson. Alloky was the head man in cracking the Brinks job."

"I didn't know they had cracked the Brinks job. I

thought some of the men and most of the money were still outstanding."

"Yeah, well Alloky's retirement came up while he was on the case so they gave him credit for cracking it. He would have if he hadn't retired; he was a real great."

This recollection of Bureau heroics seemed to recall his own, less favorable, situation. "They're not about to retire my number," he said bleakly.

"It's a tough case to draw," I commiserated.

"You're telling me. And where do you figure I sleep tonight?"

"I hadn't really given it much thought," I said. "In town?"

"Yeah, if I had bat crap for brains. What if you try to sneak out during the night? You're under twenty-four hour surveillance, which means they don't know crap about you. The way I figure it, I'm going to have to camp out in the snow like a futting Boy Scout."

"You're welcome to stay inside with me," I said. "That way you could keep me under close surveillance and be warm and comfortable."

He regarded me seriously—for signs of trickery—before agreeing with a rough Don't-Fut-with-Me look in his eyes. On the walk back to the cabin we crossed the maze of footprints which had first tipped me off to his presence.

"If this isn't classified information," I said, "do you mind telling me what you were doing out here this morning? I couldn't make any sense out of these prints."

A moment of concentration yielded a flush of embarrassment. "Oh, you know." He shrugged. "I got nothing to do so I mess around, run off a few football plays. Zazz does it all the time. Just messing around," he said lamely.

Which should give you a valuable peek in the minds of the men who are defending our country from within. If more is needed, let me add that Agent E. is presently languishing on my bed, reading *This Flogged Flesh*. He is a ravenous reader, it appears, and has gone through half my library in the space of an hour, skimming and discarding one book after another. His family is not without literary connections, he revealed to me. A few years ago his mother resided within two doors of a cousin of the author of *The Robe*. Eisentraub might even make a writer himself. He has the innately curious mind of the patiently self-destructive. Only a few minutes ago he asked me what the fut I was doing. I explained I was writing a letter. Just now he asked me to whom? In answer I gave him a brief, unflattering sketch of you; he appears to be intrigued and wishes to say a few words. The next voice you hear will be that of F.B.I. Agent Arnold Eisentraub:

> Hi, Arnie Eisentraub here.
> Now is the time for all good men to come to
> the aid of their country.

There we go. Fine sentiments for a government employee, wouldn't you say? I only wish there was time for Agent E. to wax patriotically on but, unfortunately, there are only five shopping days until Christmas and my latest sex book, *Don't Trespass on Me* is still 178 pages from completion. I have a feeling that this is not a book which can be forced onto the paper but must grow of itself, organically as it were. It is all the more difficult because I left my protagonists in a very compromising position—naked and asleep in the tall grass toward which the pastor (their father) is now leading a brigade of Sunday school children.

Which reminds me. Have you ever considered the backstage events which might be taking place during the great scenes in Literature?

...As old Barbara Frietchie pleads with Stonewall Jackson to shoot her instead of the flag, General Grant gets into his pants and makes off to the woods....

...To the rear of the train under which Anna Karenina has just flung herself, six bearded men hold the passengers at gunpoint while a seventh, a Black Russian, ravishes the younger women....

Of course, sex books are more of an outgrowth of soap operas and confession stories and the shock value is really secondary to the identification factor. Larry Strauss once showed me a fan letter he received on one of his early books, *Rape of Faith*. In the best Aristotelian tradition, the book encompassed only eight hours in the evening of a girl, Faith, who begins the evening as a virgin, is consequently kidnaped, raped, rented, forced to put on a lewd show, etc. Dawn finds her transformed into a merciless nymphomaniac driving men to their death through overexertion. The letter he got said in effect:

> I enjoyed your book very much. I thought the story was of particular interest, because the same thing happened to my sister.

By the bye, how is Sid's search for Bibbsy coming? Lovely girl, Bibbsy; sometime I'll have to write about our experiences together.

But now it is too late to do any work. Agent E. is stretching and making bedtime sounds. I shall read him his nightly chapter of *Vices of the Vikings* and then it is off to slumberland. If anyone should ask about me, please tell them I am Under Surveillance.

All love,

The Beast

DECEMBER 19

FROM DAVID NOODLEMAN

Monday

Dear Mase,
I got a million laughs out of your letter but I didn't understand a word of it. So I called Mitch to find out what the story was. He said you are very depressed and not just crazy. He said you don't like doing these dirty books really which I didn't know. If you're hung for money, why didn't you tell me? I'm spread around pretty good right now but I can always raise a couple of grand. I thought you were making a bundle on those books. Norman says he always sees a bunch of older kids reading them after school and he went up to them and said you were a personal friend of his and now they let him into their basketball games. I think the kid's a natural athlete but that makes me wonder who his father is. I told that to Cora and she said why don't I knock off twenty pounds and buy myself a set of golf clubs and maybe I'll find out. I told her I got no time for games. I wouldn't mind if the kid went into pro ball except if he was good, the fixers would get to him and if he wasn't, he'd never make a buck after he was thirty.
Listen. If it's the racket boys you're into for all this dough, I can still help you but I'd want my name kept out of it. I got enough trouble with this pizza place I bought into. Eddie Scornamie is running it. It turns out my bookie works for the racket boys that are trying to push us out so every time I lose a bet it's like throwing a rock through my window.
You must have been out of your mind to bet thirty Gs on the Colts. I don't care how many points you got. You must think Truman is still President if you think Rzeppa is any

good. Bet the Bears this week. Ocoroni's getting married. Don't give more than six.

I showed your letter to Cora's sister and she didn't think it was funny but she says she wouldn't mind meeting you. She wouldn't mind meeting anyone but that's as far as it goes. She says she's waiting for Mr. Right but what she means is Mr. Big. I wouldn't waste more than one drink on her if I was you.

I've got to end now. A Cosmo DC-6 just took out a hangar at International. I've got to get over there and see if we can get the business. I don't have any trouble giving people the business but nobody ever gives it to me. (Joke.)

Everybody sends love.

Dave

DECEMBER 20

FROM LT. COMMANDER E. B. DIBBS

THE GREAT WESTERN HOTEL
ON THE LAKE IN THE LOOP
CHICAGO, ILLINOIS

18 December

Karl,

I have moved to the above address since discovering that my nurse is in the employ of my attorneys. Please address correspondence to me here in the name of Nathan Smollett.

Do you still recommend that I retain my counsel? My telephone contact with them is worrisome. Berry appears not to recognize me. Under no circumstances give them my new address. Is there any chance of you coming here for a meeting between us.

Please reply immediately.

Smollett
(Dibbs)

P.S. Is it safe to write to you like this or are you being watched?

S.

DECEMBER 20

TO NATHAN SMOLLETT
(COMMANDER E. B. DIBBS)

Dec 20

Everett,

Thanks so much for the invitation, but unfortunately a Chicago junket is out of the question for me at the present time. Perhaps after this case is settled.

Speaking of cases, I would suggest a showdown as soon as possible. My counsel is still sluggish but he cannot be counted on to remain that way forever. A bird in the hand... as we used to say in the Gestapo.

As you guessed I am presently under surveillance but you can write to me anyway—in care of any name except Eisentraub.

Looking forward to seeing you in court soon,

Vechty

DECEMBER 22

FROM MICHAEL WESTLAKE

December 20

Dear Mase:

News. A hearing is set for December 26 in Chicago. If you haven't been served by this time, you can assume you won't be and you can start icing the champagne. Dibbs may also miss out on the festivities. He seems to have vanished. Nurse Sugar told Gru, who is back on the case, that Dibbs has been missing for five days. His seaman's bag and navigational instruments are also gone. If he's shipped out, it won't hurt our case; but then neither would his appearance. Conceivably, B. L. & G. might ask for a postponement to find him. Then again, they might feel he's more of a hindrance and go ahead without him. It's impossible to predict their next move. Perhaps they'll all retire. Berry is certainly long overdue. The B. L. & G. logbook shows that he received a few calls from Dibbs last week but he doesn't remember them.

Bibbsy remains another question mark. Sid just missed her in Barbados where she was scheduled to attend the opening of a new hotel. Her escort, a Galveston grain king, said she left the plane to get cigarettes and didn't make it back for take-off. There was a note waiting for him in Barbados saying she was okay and coming down by boat with Jojo. The grain king says he doesn't know any Jojo and did not seem happy about the whole thing. He said he doesn't know what Bibbsy's butt looks like either but he volunteered the use of his branding iron so we can put on any kind of mark we want. Since the fastest boat from Texas takes three days, all we can do is hold tight until she touches land.

As regards that gibberish of notes between you and Dibbs, enclosed please find twenty-five cents in coin and a Zippees box top for my Magic Decoder. I hope I'm the first lawyer in my firm to get one. Likewise, I don't know what to make of your essay on Eisentraub, Crapaud and Polk, Marge thinks they're real but I'm inclined to believe you made them up just to keep me from getting cocky. Or else you're suffering from hallucinations. I'll wait until I hear from you further about them before I do any checking. I'm not doubting you, you understand; just cautious.

If nothing else comes up in the interim, I'll telegram from Chicago as soon as the hearing is over and you can call and tell me what a great lawyer I am. Great lawyering is only part of it. You are undoubtedly the luckiest bastard in the world.

Mitch

DECEMBER 23

TO MICHAEL WESTLAKE

Dec 23

Dear Mitch:

They have to get up pretty early to get anything by you. Especially anything as big as Eisentraub, Crapaud and Polk. You'll be glad to know I'm all over those hallucinations now although it took some doing. For the past five days I've imagined that Eisentraub has been living with me, and that he eats like a horse. My febrile imagination supplied him with a whole dossier of characteristics from sex enthusiast to sports fiend. I kept visualizing us out in the snow at 8 a.m., thrashing through a series of push-ups, sit-ups and duck walks designed, in accordance with a training film Eisentraub had seen, to keep us fit, as well as reduce the dangers of frostbite. Following, we would stagger about in the drifts heaving Bastard's ball to and fro; then we would go on a little search for firewood. (This was my own contribution to our Olympics, but Agent E. goodnaturedly acquiesced although he recalled no such scene in the film.) This morning everything reached a climax. While we were prone in the snow, I imagined that a car stole up behind us and out came Crapaud and Polk.

"Lose something in the snow?" asked Crapaud.

"Doing exercises," said Eisentraub, pushing.

"Could have fooled me," said the chief. "I would have guessed you were having fits."

Reaching the required twenty, we got up.

"It's obvious you don't work out," said Eisentraub pointedly.

"No," said Crapaud. "I don't like to get all red in the face like that." He grinned at me. "Hello, LaDouche. How's the dirty writing coming?"

"Okay," I conceded.

"Is it true you dirty writers drink a lot of coffee?" he hinted heavily.

"No," I said. But we entered the cabin and I put up a pot anyway.

"I remember when this place was the Sheffield Sisters' whorehouse," said Crapaud reminiscently. "Hickett was chief then. I was his sergeant, no older than Polk is now. Of course I was much brighter than Polk; I was much brighter than Hickett too. He was a Lutheran, I believe. Big oxen fella, snow-white hair, but he could billygoat with the best of them. We'd come here every Thursday, after the Sheffield girls were closed to their regular customers. There wasn't room for both of us in here at once so the other would have to stand outside and talk to the other sister. The first night while I was inside, Hickett got into the car and drove off. He was a great joker. But the next time I took the spark plugs in with me and stayed for an hour listening to him trying to get the engine started. He couldn't tell a spark plug from a bee's ass, but he surely could billygoat. Amazing thing for a man that age. Had to end sometime, of course. The night it did he was in here for about two hours and when he finally came to the door he had the most disappointed look I ever saw on a man. Something beautiful had gone out of his life and he knew it was never coming back. 'Crapaud,' he said to me, and I swear to God there were tears in his eyes, 'Crapaud, go take your turn and then I'm afraid we got to close this place up.'"

"In the Bureau," said Eisentraub, "without ten or twelve years' service, you're lucky to get a futting Mann Act."

"We had ourselves a pimp not too long ago," said Crapaud. "Name of Hennegen. Said he was an atheist but I didn't believe him. He lied about everything else so I don't know why anyone'd think he'd tell the truth there. My personal opinion is that he was a Catholic but he just wouldn't admit it. You remember him, Polk?"

"No, sir."

"Yes, you do," said Crapaud. "He was the one with that suitcase full of dirty pictures you spent two days looking at. You do any of those dirty pictures?" Crapaud asked me.

"No. Not my line."

"I'd guess those guys get a little every now and then, wouldn't you say?"

"Wouldn't surprise me."

"No, it wouldn't surprise me either. Be difficult for a girl to turn you down under those circumstances. Yes, I believe it would be really hard *not* to get a piece every now and then with a job like that. That seems like the job for Polk, before he got married, of course. That is, if you could ever teach him how to use a camera. Right, Polk? Isn't that the kind of work you'd like to do?"

"No, sir. I'm happy with my job right now, sir."

"Are you really?" said Crapaud. "Isn't there something else you'd like to do?"

"No, sir."

"Nothing at all, Polk? If you had your choice of every job in the world, including keeping all those movie stars happy?"

"No, sir," said Polk.

"You're an exceptional young man, Polk," said Crapaud.

"Thank you, sir."

"I'd like to be a private detective," said Eisentraub. "Those guys really get the action."

"LaDouche," said Crapaud, "is it true that writers put whiskey in their coffee?"

"When they have whiskey," I said.

He looked ruminative. "Polk. Since you like being a policeman so much, why don't you go out to our little blue police car and bring in that bottle of Jack Daniel's that's under the floorboard."

"Yes sir," said Polk, and left.

"Zazz Stdelski and I were thinking of leaving the Bureau and opening our own detective agency," said Eisentraub. "You remember Stdelski?" he asked Crapaud. "Used to play linebacker for the Steelers."

"Ice hockey's the only sport I follow," said Crapaud. "Got interested in it about two years ago when my wife's brother got his skull fractured. Stupid fellow, Episcopalian, like my wife."

Polk returned with the bottle.

"Now then, LaDouche," said Crapaud. "I know you want to show your hospitality, and since you don't have any whiskey to offer us, I'm going to sell you this bottle for only ten dollars."

"That's a lot of money for Jack Daniel's," I said.

"This is first quality whiskey," said Crapaud.

"Are you allowed to sell liquor?" asked Eisentraub.

"In Vermont *only* the state can sell liquor," said Crapaud, like Louis XIV.

The deal was consummated and the whiskey added to the coffee of everyone but Polk.

"Now I feel truly welcome," said Crapaud. "You're a good host, LaDouche." He settled back on the bed and turned to Eisentraub. "How come you're still up here? Get lost?"

"I'm living here temporarily," said Eisentraub. "Keeping him under surveillance."

"Very clever," said Crapaud. "Hoover doesn't miss a trick."

"You take the jobs they give you," said Eisentraub.

"All depends," said Crapaud. "If they assigned you to watch your mother, would you do it?"

"They wouldn't give that to me."

"Probably not," said Crapaud, "since you'd be the best man for it. But let's say they did."

"You mean just to keep her under surveillance?"

"Umm—yes."

"Well, yes, I guess. Why not?"

"I thought so," said Crapaud. "Polk, there you have an example of a typical F.B.I. man. Not an ounce of mercy in his heart. That's the kind of man who wouldn't let a poor girl sing the Star Spangled Banner when he knew it meant everything in the world to her."

"Now, first of all," said Eisentraub, "surveillance doesn't

mean a thing. And second, you didn't say what my mother was supposed to be charged with."

"Blowing up the Pentagon," said Crapaud, filling his empty cup with whiskey and passing the bottle.

"Well, she couldn't have done it," said Eisentraub. "My mother's never been in Washington."

"Yes, she was. She was there last Sunday, when you were up here."

"How do you know?"

"Got a report over the wire on her."

"I don't believe you. What did she go down there for?"

"See the cherry blossoms," said Crapaud.

"Excuse me, sir," said Polk. "But I don't believe the cherry blossoms are in bloom in December."

"That's why she blew up the Pentagon," said Crapaud.

"I don't believe you," said Eisentraub.

Crapaud looked at him pityingly. "LaDouche, would you ever consider putting someone like him in one of your books?"

"Would you like to be in one of them?" I asked Eisentraub.

"Why not?" He grinned.

"Polk would like to be in one," said Crapaud.

"No, sir," said Polk. "I don't think I would."

"Why not?" asked Crapaud.

"Because my wife might find out about it and get the wrong idea."

"Monkey balls," said Crapaud. "It would give you prestige to have her read about you doing it ten, twelve times a night with five or six different women. Isn't that how much they usually do it in those books, LaDouche? Ten, twelve, fourteen times."

"Usually less," I said.

"Not like in real life, eh?" he said with an awful wink and reached for the bottle.

"My buddy Zazz was in a book once," said Eisentraub. "It was called 'Rookie Quarterback.' Zazz was the linebacker who crashes in and breaks the rookie quarterback's arm. He wasn't called by name, but you knew it was Zazz because he's broken quarterbacks' arms three times."

"He'd probably get along with my wife's brother," said Crapaud, sending the bottle on its way again.

The wind set up a howl that shook the cabin.

"Going to snow again," said Polk with a touch of sagacity.

"Polk's our weather expert," said Crapaud. "What do you think are the chances for a blizzard, Polk?"

"I couldn't say, sir."

"We had one helluva blizzard back about five years ago," said Crapaud. "Snow piled past the windows. I got caught in the station and, with the lines down, I couldn't even call my wife two blocks away. Not that I would have called her. I remember I had a prisoner at the time, name of Sykes. Suspected of armed robbery. Jehovah's Witness, I believe. The motel clerk saw him with a satchel full of money so we brought him in and asked him a couple of questions, but it turned out there hadn't been any hold-ups in the past few months. I was just about to let him go when the storm broke so we settled in and had a few drinks and played a little blackjack. By the time the storm let up, he was in to me for eight thousand seven hundred and forty-one dollars. Paid me right out of that satchel and left with no hard feelings. The next day we got the report on him. He was a counterfeiter." He looked up with disgust. "You play blackjack?" he asked me.

"A bit."

"Got cards?"

"No."

"Polk, do we still have those cards in the glove compartment? Took these off a sharp a while back. They're marked, but since we don't know the markings it won't make any difference. How about you, Hoover?" he asked Eisentraub. "You want to double that thirty-six-dollar-a-week paycheck?"

"I don't know what the regulations say about playing cards with suspects," said Eisentraub.

"Never if they're sharps," said Crapaud.

My desk was cleared and chairs drawn up as Polk came back with two decks and a new bottle of Jack Daniel's.

"Polk, you're going to make Chief some day," said Crapaud. "Nobody'd know it to look at you but you've got the stuff. Ten for this one too, LaDouche? No sense dickering over pennies. Dollar limit okay with everyone? Why don't I just start off dealing then."

Polk didn't play. He watched while Crapaud loudly explained the finer points until Eisentraub, who had busted three times in succession, suggested that Polk take a walk. Since it was snowing lightly then, Polk curled up on the bed instead, with Bastard beside him, and read *This Flogged Flesh*.

Pointless to mention that Crapaud did all the winning. He made a comic business about reading the marks on the cards so we could never be sure whether he could or not. Holding a fifteen, he'd squint at the back of Eisentraub's cards and say, "Damned if that doesn't look like a nineteen" (it was an eighteen), and then to the pack; "But damned if this doesn't look like a six." It was a five—enough to win without unduly inflaming our suspicions. Through luck and conservatism I managed to stay about even while Eisentraub lost with frantic consistency.

To make matters a little worse, Crapaud celebrated every other hand with a swig from the bottle and soon convinced Eisentraub that he would change his luck if he did the same. It didn't, but it increased the size of his wagers and presently he seemed to care less about losing.

"How much is it now?" he asked Crapaud after we had been playing about two hours.

"Three hundred twenty-seven dollars," said Crapaud solemnly.

"That's almost a month's salary." Eisentraub grinned stupidly.

"Then I think I'll take the next month off," said Crapaud. "Polk, how would you like to be chief for a month?"

"All right, sir. Thank you very much."

"Don't mention it. LaDouche, how would you like to be Polk's deputy?"

"I'd consider it an honor," I humored.

After a long pull on the bottle, Crapaud had a second thought. "Maybe you'd better be chief," he said to me. "Polk, you're back to sergeant again."

"Yes, sir."

Crapaud started to deal a new hand, but found he could no longer control the cards which sprayed over the table and onto the floor. He sat back lumpishly. "Never could drink in the afternoon. Hoover, you got the money you owe me?"

Eisentraub, who was not looking too good himself, seemed not to hear him. His attention was focused on Bastard, asleep beside Polk. "What kind of dog is that again?" he asked.

"Weimaraner," I said.

"Looks like a Doberman to me."

"There is a certain resemblance between the breeds," I acknowledged. "But whereas a Doberman has small erect ears, Bastard, like all other weimaraners, has loose folded ears."

"Maybe there's something wrong with his ears," said Eisentraub.

"If there is, he hasn't complained about it. He's usually very audible when in discomfort."

"Maybe he doesn't know there's something wrong with them," said Eisentraub, staring rather fixedly.

"That's possible, of course. He's not an especially intelligent animal. But there's a distinct difference in color between weimaraners and Dobermans. Weimaraners are generally gray. 'Gray ghosts' they're sometimes called, Dobermans are brown or black or occasionally blue, but never gray."

"Maybe he's a sick Doberman."

"I doubt that," I said. "There's also a dissimilarity in the shape of the head. Whereas a Doberman—"

But Eisentraub would have none of it. "That dog's a Doberman," he said. "I know it."

"No, you're mistaken. He's a weimaraner."

"Listen, if you had been bitten by as many Dobermans as I have, you'd know one when he was lying there."

"I can recognize one without having been bitten," I said.

"What about my money, Hoover?" asked Crapaud.

"Listen," Eisentraub said to me, "that dog is a Doberman pinscher. No doubt about it."

"Well, if I had any papers," I said, "I'd show them to you."

"There! So you don't have any proof he's not a Doberman."

"Do you have any proof that *you're* not a Doberman?"

That puzzled him. "What's that supposed to mean?" he asked belligerently.

"It means I'm not going to argue with you about it," I said. "I say he's a weimaraner, you say he's a Doberman. That's what makes dog racing. I don't see where it makes any great difference really."

"No? Well if he's a Doberman, I'm going to kill him." And he produced a pistol from his inside jacket pocket.

"In that case, I think we should discuss it some more," I said.

"Well discuss it after I shoot him," said Eisentraub. "I sense a certain fallacy in that procedure," I said. "What kind of dog do *you* think it is?" I asked Crapaud.

"Cocker spaniel. You got my money, Hoover?"

"Shut up," said Eisentraub hotly.

"Do you know anything about dogs?" I asked Polk.

"Not very much, sir."

"Well, would you like to offer a guess as to what kind of dog that is?"

"Well, I don't think he's a cocker spaniel. I'd say he's an Irish setter. Am I right, sir?"

"No," I said disheartened. "He's a weimaraner."

"He's a Doberman," said Eisentraub, "and I'm going to shoot him. Get out of the way," he told Polk.

"Hey," said Crapaud, whom liquor had made a little slow on the uptake, "no F.B.I. son of a bitch can tell me to shut up."

"You futting Doberman," said Eisentraub, aiming the gun at Bastard.

"Polk," said Crapaud, "disarm the prisoner."

"Yes, sir," said Polk, getting off the bed. "Surrender in the name of the law," he said to Eisentraub.

"I'm the law," said Eisentraub, "Now get out of the way."

Polk looked at Crapaud quizzically.

"Ask him if he's got my money," said Crapaud.

"Do you have the chief's money?" Polk asked.

"Get away from that dog if you don't want to get hurt," Eisentraub said.

"Put that gun away," I said.

"You want to get arrested for interfering with justice?" asked Eisentraub.

"All F.B.I. men are Communists," Crapaud generalized, his head on his chest.

"I wouldn't be an F.B.I. man if I didn't have to," said Eisentraub. "You think I like it? You think I wouldn't rather have my own detective agency with Stdelski?"

"All Stdelskis are Communists," said Crapaud to his shoes. "Polk, is the prisoner disarmed?"

"Not yet, sir."

"Stupid Baptist," said Crapaud. He stirred sluggishly. "A beautiful voice. You should have heard her sing 'Give Me Something to Remember You By.'" He looked up at me blearily. "It would have made you cry. Let's get out of here," he said to Polk.

"Yes, sir. But what about the paper, sir?"

"What paper?" said Crapaud.

"The paper we came up here to serve," said Polk.

"Get it," said Crapaud.

"I think it's in your back pocket, sir."

"I said get it!" said Crapaud. "I didn't ask where it was." He stood up and Polk came around behind him and withdrew an official-looking document, folded like a lease, from Crapaud's back pocket. Swaying perceptibly, Crapaud looked at me, then at Eisentraub, who still held the pistol at hip height aimed at Bastard. "Here, you welshing Catholic Commie," he said, and handed the paper to Eisentraub.

Eisentraub looked at it as if a pigeon had dropped it. "What the fut is this?" he said.

It was, of course, my service—with the score forty-love and Australia down three games to one in the final set here at Wimbledon....

We both inspected it for a while and then went outside to watch the police car worm down the mountain. Then Eisentraub decided to go into town to phone the Bureau and ask for advice. He returned about an hour later to say he had been instructed to 'play along with them' which meant attending the hearing in Chicago. He has reservations to leave tomorrow.

Now how's that for a hallucination, Doctor? Enough to set all Vienna on its ass, eh?

Oh, if you want Dibbs to join your merry band, you might try to reach him at the Great Western Hotel in Chicago. He is probably registered under the name of Nathan Smollett. I'm surprised a smart lawyer like you couldn't figure that out.

I suppose by now Marge has told you that she is carrying my child.

Your best friend,

Mase

DECEMBER 24

FROM BENJAMIN WINK, SPECIAL DELIVERY

December 23

Dear Mase—Just a note to check on when you got out *Trespass* if you did. We haven't received it yet. But you know what the mails are like this time of year. They don't send anything unless it's gift-wrapped, Art says. Tomorrow being Christmas Eve I don't remember whether they deliver to offices or not. But you can bet I'll be coming in to check because it won't be Christmas for me without your book. It's really getting cold here now with snow and sleet together. I told Art it might be a good time to run off a new batch of the first one you ever did for us, *Nudist Camp Tramp*. But he says he can't find the plates. But don't worry, fella, we will. Do you remember when you did that book? How times have changed. Kenny and Bill and Tony dropped in today, not to bring anything, just to say Seasons Greetings. Well it's been a big year for everyone and Merry Christmas to us all, I say. Wade right in there, boy!

Ben

DECEMBER 25

TO DAVID NOODLEMAN

Xmas

Dear Sky King:

I am writing to you on the one day which I traditionally spend only with the wife and kiddies, cavorting about the hearthside, in order to impress you with the desperation of my plight.

In God's name, why haven't I heard from you with news about what Mitch thinks I'm doing? How am I to keep up with myself if my friends don't help me? I get better service from my local F.B.I. agent who is even now filling in for me at a small legal conference. It is, I feel, a far better thing than he has ever done before.

Speaking of things, I have been busy working on a screen version of your autobiography—as much of it as I am familiar with. It was to have been a surprise for your birthday, but we ran into a casting snag. Gregory Peck is not available for the singing role of Uncle Murray. But what do you think of Frank Sinatra playing you as a young boy and Sammy Davis Jr. taking over when you turn 15? It might make for a little plot juggling but think of the box-office draw.

I hope you appreciate that this project has caused me to fall behind on my latest sex book, *Trespass Beneath Me*. It was to be under my editor's tree by Christmas morn and it is still only 22 pages done and 178 pages undone. The distributor had better wear a cup when he breaks the news to my angry readers. Mitch is really full of crap when he says I don't like doing these books. Until he started plaguing me I liked doing them fine. But Mitch has always wanted me to win the Nobel Prize because, I suspect, he has always wanted to be the friend of a Nobel Prize winner. For a time I actually thought I could make it for him but recently I have had some serious doubts. Last night, for instance, I exhumed my Three Real Books and reread them until I swooned with disgust. Each one is purely awful, as thoroughly without merit as a weed. Do you remember Phyllis Ann Betchausen, that terribly ugly, terribly stupid, terribly terrible one? Well my books are like her except they don't do it.

But how can I tell that to Mitch? It would break his heart as it almost broke mine. I feel like a greyhound who has discovered that the rabbit is electric. I know that, even running as fast as I can, I'll never catch it.

I don't think I'm feeling sorry for myself simply because I woke up this morning to find my Xmas stocking filled with soot. I think I am considering my position with beautiful objectivity. Nothing seems so useless, so expendable, and thus so pitiable, as the bad artist. He has no place; he makes no contribution. Since art survives in the masterpieces, not the mediocrities, the poor bastard's work is not only offensive but completely unnecessary. And if he's really bad enough, his efforts are never seen and no one can even profit from his blundering. He is local color, that's all. A reminder to his community that art may exist there. Be Tolerant of the Eccentric. Don't Laugh, Your Son May Be One. But for that piddling purpose the beggar doesn't even have to work at his obsession. He can just dress funny, get drunk and piss in the streets.

This letter should really be going to Mitch but I'd rather spare myself his reply. The simple truth is that I write dirty books because it's what I can do. And because it pays well. So I really don't need any bread right now, but thanks for the offer. I'm not the type to give in to the racket boys, anyway. I'd rather change my face and run.

Now I must change my ribbon and get on with *Bypass Around Me,* my latest sex dirge. Mitch thinks that my editor, Wink, is Satan in disguise but he is really closer to Santa. Without his myopic admiration, I would probably perish. If I ever amass a superfluous fortune I am going to commission Monty to build a library in Wink's honor. In the anteroom a bronze plaque will show a frieze of Wink at his desk perusing a manuscript. (If a photo is unavailable, tell Monty to use Winston Churchill; they are look-a-likes.) Below the frieze, the raised inscription will read:

In Honor of Benjamin Wink
Editor of Scepter Books

"He Did So Much to Keep
the Kids off the Streets"

I may also throw up a small statue to you when you score 500. Or maybe I'll just sneak up and bronze you in medias res.

In the spirit of the season,

Your Brother Grim

DECEMBER 27

FROM MICHAEL WESTLAKE, TELEGRAM

HEARING OVER KVPXLL DNAES RDUTYMG
LETTER TO FOLLOW

MITCH

FROM MICHAEL WESTLAKE,
SPECIAL DELIVERY

Mase,

This is being written en route to my home, my bed and my hot little wife. Since there will be no transcript, there is a great deal to get down before I do. However, when that seat belt sign flashes, finished or not, I am going to set down my pen; when I reach the first mail box I am going to post this and thereafter I will never mention the case again. Never. If Marge happens to bring it up, I will merely smile and connubial her; if any other good-looking women bring it up, I will smile and adulterate them; if a man brings it up, I will leave the room; if you ever mention it, I will coldcock you.

Here is the blow by blow:

I arrived in Chicago at 11:07 this morning. The hearing was set for 1 p.m. Mostly for the hell of it, I called the Great Western and asked for Nathan Smollett. I felt consummately foolish doing so and even more so when he answered. Our conversation ran like this:

"Smollett?"

"Yes."

"Dibbs?"

"Yes. Vechtenmeisser?"

"No. Westlake."

"Who?"

"Westlake. Greer's lawyer."

"Gru?"

"No. Greer. Vechtenmeisser."

At last we established identities and he sounded very glad that I had arrived. Things were going very badly. Did I know that Gru and Berry had a secret conference planned for that afternoon? He had found out from Nurse Sugar. When I told him I was aware of their plan and was going to attend the meeting, he was gleeful. He had not planned on going

because that would play right into Gru's hands'; instead he
had recruited the hotel night clerk, a man named Ziffren
who had served with him in the South Pacific, to act as his
representative. He assured me that Ziffren was a top-notch
sailor as well as a good man with an anti-aircraft gun.

I began to feel as you had that this man was a certifiable
lunatic. I also realized how much his appearance could
help our case. I tried to convince him to attend, dwelling
on the dangers inherent in letting B. L. & G. run the case
unsupervised. He countered by asking if I would represent
him. I told him the courts would not look kindly upon me
acting as counsel for both sides, that it would smack of
monopoly. I intimated that the meeting had all the earmarks
of a turning point and that we would all feel better with
his steady hand at the helm. I'm not sure why I said that.
Talking to Dibbs is a little like descending in an unstoppable
elevator at top speed. In any case, he agreed to come, and
to bring Ziffren too. We made plans to meet in the lobby of
the Great Western at 12:30.

I was there at 12:25. A fattish, fiftyish, baldish man
wearing a sailor suit was behind the desk. When I asked him
if he might be Mr. Ziffren, he pulled himself together and
saluted: "Chief Bosun's Mate Ziffren, Loren S. reporting for
duty, sir."

I put him at ease and asked where Dibbs was. He said the
commander had gone ashore for a moment but would be
back directly. We waited in awkward silence. Finally Ziffren
asked me if I had been in the service. I admitted to the Judge
Advocate's Corps. "Better not tell that to the old man," he
advised. "He's hell on desk sailors."

Presently the old man appeared. He looks like Ty Cobb,
wore dress whites and carried a swagger stick which he
used as both cane and crop. He greeted me heartily, said he
was glad to have me aboard. While Ziffren was out getting
us a cab, Dibbs confided that he had been late because he
had been out buying new epaulets. His old ones didn't take
a shine any more. "It may not seem like much," he said
without a trace of humor, "but that's the type of thing that

can destroy the crew's morale." He went on to laud Ziffren's fine record. In the cab he asked me in what branch of the military I had served. I said paratroopers. "Couldn't have done it without them," he said.

The hearing was held in the small claims court of the Justice Building. We arrived twenty minutes late. The judge's name was Lask, a small, wry man who seemed to realize the impossibility of concepts like Law or Justice. When he inquired of our delay and I explained I had just located the plaintiff, he said, "You mean the defendant, don't you, counselor?"

"No, your Honor," I said. "The plaintiff."

"Aren't you the counsel for the plaintiff?"

"Yes, your honor."

"I see. That is, I don't see. But I have every confidence that I shall."

I settled in and organized my motion for immediate dismissal while the stenographer read the complaint. The courtroom looked just like the kind you see on television. At the table across from me sat Gru, a cool, incompetent young man with swimming contact lenses. He was happily whispering to Dibbs who looked none too happy to be there. On the other side of Dibbs sat senile old Berry, trying to look necessary by squaring his stack of blank notepaper. Behind them, in the first row, sat Ziffren, looking alert; your old friend Lock: stolid, angry and apparently permanently resigned in a sport coat and pink shirt; and, finally, your colleague, Dr. Quinones: continental, mustached, searching for a handkerchief.

On our side, in the row behind me, was Crapaud, dressed like a tourist farmer, and Eisentraub, whom I would have recognized anywhere. We exchanged introductions, hands were shaken and I asked Crapaud why he had come.

"Just for the ride," he said. "The county is paying. Never been to Chicago. Certainly smells like the world's hog butchery."

"Anything you want me to do?" Eisentraub asked me. Apparently he thought I was his temporary superior. I merely reminded him that his testimony would be considered as under oath and to answer all questions truthfully.

"Bureau agents are always under oath," he said.

"They're under everything," said Crapaud. "Is this going to take long?" he asked me. "I could stand a drink."

I told him I expected it would be over in a matter of minutes, and as soon as the stenographer completed the statement, I rose snappily and requested an immediate dismissal on the grounds of improper service. I documented the impropriety as Gru looked stunned.

Lask looked impressed. "Very able, counselor," he said. "Looks like we're in for an early afternoon. Do you have anything to say to that?" he asked Gru. "Has the defendant been served?"

"Yes, your Honor. A bonded police officer of the state of Vermont served him. Captain Crapaud, was the complaint served?"

"It surely was," Crapaud smiled.

Gru looked at me with disdain.

"But not to the defendant," I said. "The complaint was served to this man." I pointed to Eisentraub.

"And who might he be?" asked Lask.

"An agent of the F.B.I.," I said.

"And a Catholic Communist," put in Crapaud.

"Is that true?" Lask asked Eisentraub.

"The part about the Bureau is," said Eisentraub.

"State your full name and occupation, please," said Lask.

"Arnold Mordecai Eisentraub, Special Agent, Federal Bureau of Investigation."

"Rah, rah, rah," said Crapaud.

Lask looked at him indulgently. "Have you been drinking, Captain?"

"Since I was seven," said Crapaud.

Lask smiled. "Strike that from the record," he told the stenographer, and turned back to Eisentraub. "Now, Mr. Eisentraub, am I to understand that you accepted a complaint which was intended for the defendant?"

"Yes, sir."

"Might I ask why?"

"Yes. I didn't know what it was."

"What did you think it was?"

"I didn't know."

"But you thought it was for you?"

"Yes."

"Did the officer address you by name when he handed you the paper?"

"No."

"What did he say?"

"He said 'Here, you welshing Catholic Commie.'"

"Strike 'Commie' from the record," Lask instructed the stenographer. "And strike my saying it too," he added. He turned to Crapaud. "Captain, did you know that Agent Eisentraub was not the defendant when you served him?"

"Damn right."

"But you served him anyway."

"Yeah."

"Might I ask why?"

"The red bastard deserved it."

"Strike that," said Lask calmly.

"Your Honor," said Gru, "I suggest that the plaintiff cannot be held responsible for the irresponsibility of the officer entrusted to serve the complaint."

"A good point," said Lask. "Counselor," he said to me, "is the real defendant here?"

"No, your Honor."

"Might I ask why?"

"He was never served, your Honor."

"Another good point."

"Your Honor," said a new voice. Quinones rose from his seat. "Your Honor, I suggest that the defendant *is* here."

"Are you he?" asked Lask.

"No, your Honor. I am Dr. Pietro Quinones."

"How do you do, Doctor. Now will you please sit down so we can get on with this hearing." He turned back to Gru and me. "It seems to me, gentlemen, that if the service was improper, there are grounds for a dismissal here. However, since it appears..."

Berry, into whose ear Quinones had been whispering, now rose. "Your Honor," he said, smiling benignly.

"Yes, counselor." Lask smiled back, respecting age.

"Your Honor," said Berry.

"Yes."

"Your honor." His smile faded to blankness. He turned to Quinones. "What was it you said again?" Quinones whispered violently.

"Oh yes," said Berry. "Your Honor—" He smiled. "With your permission, it has been suggested by Dr. Simpson—"

"Quinones," Quinones rasped sharply.

"—that Mr. Quinones is actually present in the courtroom. I would ask that Dr. Simpson be given a chance to speak."

"All right," said Lask, amused. "Dr. Simpson."

"Quinones, your Honor," said Quinones. "Dr. Pietro Quinones." He grinned toothily and patted his mustache. "With your Honor's indulgence, in the past month I have had the opportunity to conduct some psychiatric tests on the defendant. Although these tests were by mail and I have never met the defendant in person, I have come to feel that I know him well. It is my conclusion, as a result of these tests, that the defendant is a psychopathic liar with exhibitionistic tendencies. Thus, it is not unlikely that he is in this courtroom right now, masquerading under an assumed name, glorying in the spectacle of his own debasement."

"Really," said Lask. "Would you care to point him out for us?"

"Gladly, your Honor," said Quinones. It is my belief that *that* is the defendant!" And he pointed at Eisentraub.

Crapaud nearly fell from his chair laughing.

"An interesting theory, Doctor," said Lask, "but unfortunately that gentleman has already been identified as F.B.I. Agent Eisenstrobe. Mr. Eisenstrobe, for the record, again, would you please state your name and occupation."

"Arnold Mordecai Eisentraub, Special Agent, Federal Bureau of Investigation."

"Hip, hip, hooray," said Crapaud.

"Oh, why don't you go fut yourself!" said Eisentraub.

"Strike that," said Lask.

"You have a speech impediment?" Crapaud asked Eisentraub.

"Fut you," Eisentraub said very distinctly.

"Strike that," said Lask.

"Excuse me," said the stenographer, "but how is that spelled?"

"You little pinko," said Crapaud, rising.

"Strike that," said Lask. "Gentlemen, I—"

"Call me a Commie again," said Eisentraub, "and—"

"Commie," said Crapaud.

"Strike that," said Lask. "Gentlemen, I am giving you first and last warning—"

"Call me a Commie again," said Eisentraub.

"Commie."

"Excuse me," said the stenographer.

"—before," said Lask, "I will hold you both in—"

"Once more," said Eisentraub. "Just once more."

"Commie!"

"Contempt!" said Lask, smashing with the gavel and signaling to two guards who descended upon Crapaud and Eisentraub.

"Oh, forget it," said the stenographer.

"I find you both guilty of contempt," said Lask as Eisentraub and Crapaud were wheeled by him. "And sentence you to serve three days in jail." He rapped the gavel as the door slammed behind them. "Now, gentlemen, without meaning to sound impatient, I wonder if we could proceed with the hearing proper. Are you finished, Doctor?"

"I cannot believe it," said Quinones, shaking his head and walking slowly to the rear door. "All the symptoms. Very strange."

"Counselor," Lask said to Gru. "Is the plaintiff here?"

"Yes, your Honor."

"Will you please introduce him now for the purposes of questioning?"

"Certainly, your Honor. Lt. Commander E. B. Dibbs, United States Navy, Retired."

Dibbs snapped to attention as did Ziffren beside him.

Lask looked amused. "How do you do, Commander? I see you've brought your own honor guard."

"Your Honor, may I present Chief Bosun's Mate Ziffren, Loren S."

"A pleasure," said Lask. "Now, Commander, could you tell me about this alleged libel, how it came to your attention, et cetera."

"I have nothing to say at this time, your Honor."

"Oh?" said Lask.

"The dispute between the defendant and myself is an international one and should be decided in an international court of law."

"Is your client all right, counselor?" Lask asked Gru.

Gru looked confused. "I'm sorry, your Honor. But if I may, I'd like to have a minute to consult with my client."

"How would a recess sound?" asked Lask.

"Very good, your Honor."

"Ten years be long enough?" asked Lask.

Gru colored.

"Counselor," said Lask, "if your client does not wish to prefer charges, I'm afraid I must dismiss this case. Commander Dibbs, am I to understand that you do not wish to prefer charges?"

"At the proper time and to the proper authorities," said Dibbs.

"Fine," said Lask. "I'll be looking forward to reading about it in the papers. Gentlemen, if that is all..."

"What about the rocks?" said a hoarse voice. It was Lock, rising, red-faced. "Who's going to pay for the rocks that son of a bitch sent me?"

"Strike that," said Lask wearily. "Counselor—" he addressed Gru—"is this gentleman a member of your contingent?"

"Yes, your Honor. He's an associate counselor."

"Arresting courtroom manner," said Lask.

"He kept sending me rocks," said Lock.

"Who?" asked Lask.

It was at that point that a bailiff came in and whispered to Lask. "Mr. Westlake," Lask said.

"Yes, your Honor."

"Do you know a Mr. Sidney Polsky?"

"Yes, your Honor."

"Well, he's just called to inform you that a Bibbsy Dibbs has married a Karl Vechtenmeisser. Does that mean anything to anyone?"

It meant something to Dibbs, who immediately dropped all charges. He wouldn't think of suing his new son-in-law. Hearing that, Lask dismissed the hearing and left so quickly that no one even had a chance to rise. Dibbs, with Ziffren trailing, rushed out to try to contact the happy couple while I left to call Sid, leaving Gru and Lock looking like something in Madame Tussaud's. But Berry remained cheerful. Looking around the emptying courtroom, he said, "Recess, eh? Good thinking, lad, good thinking."

Sid gave me the details of the nuptials which were held at Squaw Valley that morning. It seems that Bibbsy and Karl bumped into each other by accident and love flamed up like cellophane. Bibbsy told Sid they are going to have a baby but this may just be bridal expectation and not a *fait accompli*. Although sentimental, Sid is enough of a lawyer to have arranged for a complete release to be in Bibbsy's hands within the hour. In exchange, a wedding present of a portable bar was sent to them in your name. The cost will be included in our fee which, as near as I can figure, should run about $120,000.

There goes the seat belt sign.

DECEMBER 28

FROM MR. AND MRS. S. BONKERS, CARD

Mr. and Mrs. Stuart Bonkers
announce the marriage of their daughter
Natalie Jewell
to
Mr. Wallace Corey Cooms
Sunday, the twenty-third of December
North Highlands, New Jersey

DECEMBER 29

FROM DAVID NOODLEMAN

Friday

Dear Mase,

If you ask me, I'm right and Mitch is wrong. You're crazy. That was the most depressing letter I ever got. I wanted to throw it away and forget I ever saw it, but Cora read it and said if I was a friend of yours I should write something to cheer you up. I'm a friend but I don't know what to write. Maybe all that cold has got to your brain and you should come down to Miami and sit in the sun for a few weeks.

We've got news here which is that Cora's sister may be pregnant. She's a week late and has stopped kidding about it. She won't even tell Cora who the guy is, and personally, I think it's like picking All-Americans. Like I always said, when a broad tells you No, she's telling some other guy Yes. But if she doesn't get married, I see her as an easy touch for someone like you who plays his cards right. Also my cousin Estelle is coming down to stay with us sometime in February. That's the one bad thing about Miami. In winter the relatives never let you alone. Still this could be good news because Estelle always had it for me. But I read somewhere that you can get a blood disease by making it with a relative. But didn't Coolidge marry his niece?

I have the feeling this is not going to cheer you up very much and it is only depressing me. What have I got to tell you except that I am going to get laid tonight even if it's only Cora and I think you should do the same?

Dave

P.S. I sent your letter to Mitch. If I wasn't a friend, I wouldn't have told you.

DECEMBER 31

FROM LT. COMMANDER E. B. DIBBS

29 December

Dear Son,

It was good of you and Barbara to call yesterday. I had tried to reach you the day before but the Camphor operator would not give me your listing. I hope you will forgive an old man his display of sentiment. Barbara will tell you I am not often guilty of such unmilitary behavior. But those were tears of happiness for you both. We have had our differences, Karl, but only under adversity are men truly revealed. I have come to admire your spirit, your courage and now, your honor. Someday I must tell you how Barbara's mother and I came to be wed.

Although it embarrasses me to admit it, son, I enjoyed your little novel very much. Undisputedly, you have talent, and whether you wish to use it with the pen or with the poles, I know you will be a great success and a source of pride to Barbara and me. I look forward to shaking your hand and delivering these sentiments personally when the season is over and you and Barbara come home.

God bless you, son, and take good care of our little girl.

Fondly,
Dad Dibbs

P.S. Is your father still living? Does he ever get over to this country? If so, I'd certainly enjoy meeting him and exchanging military experiences.

JANUARY 2

FROM MICHAEL WESTLAKE

December 30

Dear Mase:

This will be brief because Marge just called to say it's time we had another child.

I arrived here to find a note from Dave. I don't have it at hand but I think I recall its substance:

> Mitch,
> What does this mean?
> Dave

Enclosed was your Christmas letter to him. I am enclosing it herewith simply because I don't know what else to do with it. I surely don't want it. Why don't you send it back to Dave? Also enclosed please find a photostat of a release pertaining to some legal matter, three thousand pieces of related correspondence and my bill. The latter is the only item I commend to your immediate attention. If payment is not received within ten days, you shall hear from my attorneys, Berry, Lock & Gru.

(As a final addendum to all that, Crapaud and Eisentraub received suspended sentences; undoubtedly it is the first time in the history of jurisprudence that a police department and the F.B.I. posted bond.)

Now, idiot. The purpose of a bad writer is the same as that of a good writer and everyone else in the world: to do the best he can. If he accomplishes something monumental, fine; but it is the work that is his real function and it is the dream of greatness that really matters. Even Polk knows that. It's why he doesn't want to hear your books are fiction. It's also why Crapaud keeps hoping for that letter from Hoover and why a frustrated old Navy commander hunts imaginary Nazis and why Dave tries to score 500 and Eisentraub sticks with the Bureau and Wink thinks you're one of the greats.

It's even why I hope to make some unique contribution to the concept of law. But if I ever did, I'd want to make another, bigger one the next day. Just as if Dave ever hit 500, he'd shoot for 1000. And the same with all the others.

Don't you see that you can't write trash books any more because they're not worth writing and because you've shown you can do it? Aim for the Nobel if you like, but don't do it to please me. Confidentially, it's not a famous novelist I've always wanted for a pal, it's a pope. But whether I like it or not, you happen to be a writer. When you come right down to it, you're completely un-suited for anything else. So you might as well stop bitching and write.

You can start with a check to me.

Mitch

FROM BENJAMIN WINK

December 30

Dear Mase—Just a note to tell you I'm not worried about the book. I know there must be some good reason for the delay if it hasn't been lost in the mails. I won't even mention it again. When you get it done, fella, just send it along. We all have our bad days so don't be ashamed. Just to show you my confidence, I've got a little surprise for you. Strapper Books has come out with a new line that is sweeping the market. Phony case histories and interviews written by fake doctors. Some of them have been called *The L-------n*, *The H--------l* and *The Sex P-----t*. Bill and Kenny are now doing some for us on *The N-------c*, *the M-------t* and *The S-----t*, and if they can do it, fella, you can do it that much better. I wanted you to know about it before all the good subjects are gone so if you have a favorite, drop me a line and I'll save it for you. And, as if the money made any difference, I think there'll be twice as much in it as the old stuff. Just a little something to whet your appetite. But now I can't wait for you to be finished with *Trespass*. Swing from the floor, fella! And a Happy New Year!

Ben

FROM ROBERT J. HAYES, *WILKINS COMMERCIAL*, WILKINS, MD.

December 30

Dear Mr. Greer:

In reply to your letter of December 11, it is not our policy to fill requests for back issues prior to one month from the date of the request. The article to which you referred appeared in the *Commercial* on October 9 of this year.

In reply to your request for specific information concerning Mr. Spragg, the article was a feature following his death by heart attack upon hearing he had won first prize of $500 in the *Commercials* prizewords Contest. Mr. Spragg was 87, a veteran of World War I and an Elk.

I hope this information will be of some help to you. Thank you for your interest in our newspaper and for your small check which has been contributed to our Better Books Fund.

All best wishes,

Robert J. Hayes, Editor

JANUARY 5

TO BENJAMIN WINK, COVER LETTER TO PARCEL

Jan 5

Dear Ben:

Enclosed please find my latest book. As you can see it is only 22 pages long. This is not because it is an extraordinarily short book; it is because it is an unfinished book. I, however, am finished with it. It is yours to do with as you wish. I am retiring from the pornography game. But if you have someone complete the book, as a last gesture I would suggest that the title be changed. As it stands the biblical association might offend some of the touchier sects. You might call it *Do Unto Others.*

I hope you understand that my decision to retire is based on personal reasons and does not reflect upon you or the organization. I shall always be grateful to Scepter in the way that a child is grateful for a Mammy; as far as my fondness for you, let me mention that recently I suggested that a library be built in your honor. I feel you are a truly good man, albeit one who may be deceived as to his intentions. I would not consider altering those intentions but I feel I must remove myself as a means of achieving them.

I know you will have some interest in my future plans. At the present time several attractive offers have been tended me. The most promising is the job of librettist for the upcoming musical based on the life of the Marquis de Sade. If all goes well, it should be on the boards next fall under the title *Mean to Me.* I know you wish me well in my new endeavors as I do you in yours. We shall each, I hope, keep punching!

Mase

JANUARY 10

FROM BENJAMIN WINK

January 8

Dear Mase—Just a note in answer to yours of January 5. I can't tell you how bad I feel about you not finishing *Do Unto*. The book is absolutely great as far as it goes. Your best yet, boy. Art wants Bill or Tony to wrap it up for you but I won't let those hacks touch it. It's here waiting for you whenever you want to go back to it. Hope it's soon. I almost cried when I read about that library you're building for me. But the only library I want is one of your books. You know I wish you all the luck in the world with your new show and I'll be the first one on line for tickets when it opens. Maybe we can publish it in book form. Or, if it's mostly songs, put out a record. There's a big audience for that, too. But I have the feeling that Broadway can't hold a great like you for very long. And when that time comes, I'll be glad to have you back on the team. Stay in a crouch, fella!

Ben

About the Author

Hal Dresner has written teleplays (for *Night Gallery, M*A*S*H,* and *The Harvey Korman Show*), screenplays (*Catch 22, The Eiger Sanction,* and *Zorro, the Gay Blade*) and short stories (many collected in various Alfred Hitchcock anthologies). He has also cowritten, under a pseudonym, several softcore erotic novels. Most of his work has humorous elements, and he was widely acclaimed for his comic novel *The Man Who Wrote Dirty Books.*

OPEN ROAD
INTEGRATED MEDIA

Open Road Integrated Media is a digital publisher and multimedia content company. Open Road creates connections between authors and their audiences by marketing its ebooks through a new proprietary online platform, which uses premium video content and social media.

CPSIA information can be obtained
at www.ICGtesting.com
Printed in the USA
JSHW010228110620
6167JS00003B/110